Praise for *The Puppeteer's Daughters*

"Heartfelt, intriguing and breathtakingly creative. *The Puppeteer's Daughters* proves that happily-ever-afters aren't always the ending to fairytales—sometimes they're just the beginning. Heather Newton is a born storyteller, showing us that magic can spill into our everyday lives when we step out of our comfort zones." —**Sarah Addison Allen**, *New York Times* **bestselling author of** *Garden Spells and Other Birds*

"Beautifully rooted in classic fairy tales, and rich with the intricacies of the puppeteer's art, Heather Newton's novel animates the lives of three complex women." —**Laura Kalpakian, author of** *Memory Into Memoir* **and** *These Latter Days*

"*The Puppeteer's Daughters* by Heather Newton masterfully captures the tenderness and tension between sisters . . . Newton employs a light touch with this enchanting tale of memory, myth, and magic, as each of *The Puppeteer's Daughters* begins to untangle her complicated family legacy." —**Kim Wright, author of** *The Canterbury Sisters* **and** *Last Ride to Graceland*

"Heather Newton has crafted engaging female characters on powerful personal transformative journeys, whilst opening a window into the rich, yet secluded world of puppetry and creativity." —**Sara Alexander,** *Under a Sardinian Sky*

"With their charismatic but flawed father in decline, sisters Rosie, Jane, and Cora must come to terms with old hurts and heartaches as they sort out his legacy to them—and what they owe each other. Heather Newton has written a tender fami prose, a lot of heart, some big secrets, and —**Sarah McCraw Crow, author of** *The Wr*

"*The Puppeteer's Daughters* brings us into the world of puppetry and fairytales, rivalries and love stories, both through tales interwoven throughout the novel and in the lives of a family of sisters, who must suddenly redefine who they are to one another. This book is perfectly plotted, wonderfully paced, with characters I loved and rooted for page after page. Newton excellently weaves individual narratives of the daughters' as they navigate their own journeys alongside the shifting dynamics of the sisters as a whole, all the while delighting us with the intricacies of puppetry, from the classic tales themselves to the mechanics of how to bring the little wooden bodies to life. I love this book." —**Tessa Fontaine, author of** *The Electric Woman: A Memoir in Death-Defying Acts*

"*The Puppeteer's Daughters* is the unflinching human tale of three sisters navigating their relationships to an ailing father, who is often as loving as he is punitive. Here is a story of fairy tales, puppetry, and a dash of mystery that will wrap you up in warmth and tender familiarity. It is extraordinary in its exploration of the beautiful and often fragmented bond between siblings, and will immediately entrance you through tiny glimpses into their heartache, joy, loss, and redemption. This is the family saga we all need right now." —**Carmen Ritter, Malaprop's Bookstore/Cafe**

"In *The Puppeteer's Daughters*, Heather Newton has reimagined King Lear as a modern-day Jim Henson style creative genius. But unlike Lear, Walter Gray has an unacknowledged fourth daughter whose existence adds to the plot twists. Recommended for fans of Jane Smiley." —**Jill Hendrix, owner of Fiction Addiction**

The Puppeteer's Daughters

Also by Heather Newton

McMullen Circle
Under The Mercy Trees

The Puppeteer's Daughters

a novel

Heather Newton

KEYLIGHT
BOOKS
AN IMPRINT
OF TURNER
PUBLISHING

Keylight Books

an imprint of Turner Publishing Company

Nashville, Tennessee

www.turnerpublishing.com

Cover design by Lauren Peters-Collaer

Text design by William Ruoto

Library of Congress Cataloging-in-Publication Data

Names: Newton, Heather, author.

Title: The puppeteer's daughters / by Heather Newton.

Description: Nashville, Tennessee : Keylight Books, an imprint of Turner
  Publishing Company, [2022]

Identifiers: LCCN 2021042131 (print) | LCCN 2021042132 (ebook) | ISBN
  9781684428588 (hardcover) | ISBN 9781684428595 (paperback) | ISBN
  9781684428601 (ebook)

Classification: LCC PS3614.E75 P87 2022 (print) | LCC PS3614.E75 (ebook)
  | DDC 813/.6—dc23

LC record available at https://lccn.loc.gov/2021042131

LC ebook record available at https://lccn.loc.gov/2021042132

Printed in the United States of America

For my father, Carl Newton. My hands are like your

hands. And for my mother, Suzanne Newton, who

showed me how to claim a creative life.

"*You marionettes, you my beloved dolls, you playthings of the mind . . .*"

— PIERRE GAUCHAT

In fairy tales, father-kings act in anger, only to regret it later.

His daughters had some nerve, placing conditions on his driving. He'd teach them about conditions.

He slid his will from its sheath. He found paper and wrote the word "Codicil" at the top, feeling the power in his pen strokes. He was the Puppeteer, leaning over the rail, hands spread as he orchestrated his daughters' lives.

The condition on Jane's inheritance was easy and satisfying. His pen tip tore paper. It was harder for Cora, his favorite, but he would show her too. As for Rosie, she might be innocent, but why should he exempt her from his control?

The frenetic scratch of *t*'s crossed and periods stabbed shredded the silence of his study. When he finished, he stapled the addendum to his will and sat back, ready to enjoy what he had done. His gypsy princess marionette, the first puppet he ever made himself, hung from a hook near his desk where he sometimes manipulated her when mulling a creative problem, using her the way some people used worry beads to help himself think. In the dim light, her painted expression seemed to chide him.

A profound fatigue overtook him. He was not in control of his girls. They had left him. They were their own people. His angry scribbling only made him feel ashamed.

"Don't look at me like that," he told the puppet. "I'll destroy it when I'm over my snit."

He put the will away and dragged himself to bed. In the morning, he remembered the codicil as he settled the gypsy princess in his suitcase, but his mind was rotten cloth that one couldn't mend without more tearing—new holes opened up where the needle entered. The will with its conditions stayed where he'd filed it. He never thought of it again.

Chapter 1

I n the dining room of the Bevins Estate nursing home, Jane and the caterers decorated for her father's eightieth birthday party, balloon-bunch centerpieces on each table featuring the puppets from his *Zeno and Friends* television show.

A reporter from the local CBS affiliate where her father got his start was pre-taping a segment for the national news: "From his earliest marionettes to his iconic Emmy award–winning children's show *Zeno and Friends*, we celebrate renowned puppeteer Walter Gray today on his eightieth birthday and the thirty-fifth anniversary of *Zeno and Friends*. Generations of Americans have grown up with Zeno. Mr. Gray has been out of the public eye for some years now, but we know our viewers will wish him well."

The reporter lowered his mic. "When will your sisters get here? I want a shot of Mr. Gray with all of you."

"Half-sisters," Jane corrected. "Rosie better come soon— she made the cake. Cora's flying in."

"It must've been cool to grow up with Walter Gray for a dad," the reporter said.

"I guess," said Jane.

🪶

AT THE NEW YORK CITY HEADQUARTERS OF GRAY STEED PUP-pets, Cora strode down the hall with her vice president,

Alice Cannady. Around them, puppeteers practiced choreography, store rooms spilled puppet parts and fur, and a small explosion erupted from a prop room.

"If you're lucky, the storm won't delay your flight." Alice handed Cora a bulging scrapbook. "These are well wishes from Walter's fellow puppet masters. And before you go I need your signature on the Mattel contract for the new toy line."

Cora stopped walking. "I wasn't impressed with the prototypes. Cheap-looking."

"I know, but the sales will fund the next five years of the Puppet Lab. Creativity has its price."

Cora had founded the Walter Gray Puppet Lab in honor of her father, to provide fellowships to emerging avant-garde puppeteers. She signed the contract with reluctance and ran for the elevator.

"Give my love to your dad!" Alice called.

*

ROSIE STRUGGLED OUT THE DOOR OF HER HOUSE, CARRYING a large sheet cake decorated with her father's most famous puppet, Zeno, whose spiky hair she'd captured in sky blue icing. Rosie's Sunday dress and even her heels felt tighter than the last time she'd tried them on. She handed her five-year-old daughter, Madison, off to her ex, Gary. "Be good at Daddy's house, Madison."

Madison bounced on her toes. "Save me a piece of cake!"

"If it gets eaten, I'll make a new one just for you."

Gary opened the passenger side door of his truck so Madison could scramble in. "Hey, how about we fool around after the party?" he said to Rosie.

"What about your girlfriend?" she asked.

"Amber don't have to know about it."

"I can't. Jane wants us to pack up Dad's things. They're transferring him from assisted living to nursing care today." A few years earlier, Jane had moved their father into a gracious assisted living suite at the Bevins Estate, putting a stop to his jumbled finances, missed medications, and him reporting his car stolen from various parking lots. The Bevins staff adored him and had covered for him as long as they could, but his dementia was progressing and he was losing bladder and bowel control. The director of nursing had decided he needed a higher level of care.

"Jane's plan is to just not take him back to his suite after the party." Rosie shifted the cake on her hip. "He won't even remember."

AT BEVINS, JANE FRETTED AS GUESTS BEGAN TO SHOW UP FOR the party, until Rosie finally arrived. Breathless, Rosie set the cake on a table and checked her phone. "Cora's on her way from the airport."

"She should have come sooner." *Zeno and Friends* had made Cora rich, not Jane. Cora should have been the one spending hours setting up the silly Zeno party decorations.

An aide brought their father in, holding his elbow as he shuffled over to Jane and Rosie. Guests applauded and he waved to them. He pointed with delight at the Zeno cake Rosie had made. "Look at that! Look at that . . . whatnot. His name is . . . His name is . . ."

"It's Zeno, Dad," Jane said impatiently. He was losing his words. *Pencil* had become "that thing that is long that makes marks." *Sandwich* was "that thing with bread and whatnot." Jane braced for the day when she would cease to be *Jane* and become "that old girl who comes here and frowns."

"Zeno! Of course it is," Walter said.

Rosie led Walter to an armchair. "Have a seat, Dad, so people can come say hi."

Cora swept in, smelling of winter. She went straight to Walter and kissed the top of his head. "Hi Dad, sorry I'm late."

Walter's face lit up.

"About time," Jane said.

"My flight was the last one they allowed out. Hoping the storm won't hit until the party's over." Cora shed her coat.

Guests, including children, lined up to wish Walter a happy birthday.

The reporter had prepared a montage of vintage clips that looped on a large screen behind the punch bowl. In blurry low definition, Walter's early wolf marionette chased Red Riding Hood. Jack climbed a beanstalk. A gypsy queen whispered a secret in her small daughter's ear. Walter's stringed weatherman, Partley Cloudy, mouthed off to the station's meteorologist, earning canned laughter. Then, vibrant in high definition, came the puppets from the most recent *Zeno and Friends* special. Live-handed and large, they dwarfed the marionettes they had replaced.

"Let's get some shots of Mr. Gray with you girls." The reporter grabbed a plush Zeno puppet from a little boy showing off to Walter how he could sing the theme song to *Zeno and Friends*.

"Jane, you're the eldest—hold Zeno," the reporter instructed. His cameraman readied the shot.

Jane wouldn't touch the puppet. "Let Cora hold it. She's the heir apparent."

"Even better," the reporter said.

Cora slipped her hand inside Zeno and made him wave to the crowd. Their father chortled.

Rosie hovered off to the side. "Get in the frame, Rosie," Cora said, but Rosie's weight these days was above three hundred pounds. She had to stand behind their father's chair so she didn't obscure him.

Once the reporter and cameraman left with their footage, Cora returned the Zeno puppet to its tearful owner. More partygoers lined up to wish Walter well. He was jovial with his guests—old friends from the days when his marionettes performed fairy tales, and parents with children who knew only his foam characters.

Sleet tapped on the windows but the dining room remained cozy. As the cake got eaten and the crowd thinned, the aide signaled that Walter's new room was ready. To distract him she asked, "Are these all your children?"

"This is us," Jane said.

"No," Walter said. "There's another one."

His girls looked at each other. "You're tired, Dad," Cora said.

The aide helped him stand. Walter resisted their attempts to point him down the hall. "I have four daughters. Where is she? Where's the other one?"

Jane couldn't hide her irritation. "Three, Dad. Count us. Three."

Chapter 2

Jane had him first, during the itinerant Volkswagen camper years and then in the suburban split-level they couldn't afford on Ginkgo Street. He chose the house for its walk-in basement, with room for a curtained stage and an entrance the audience could use without traipsing through the upstairs. He hung his marionettes lovingly backstage, seeing to their comfort before his family's. On a street of conforming homes, he painted their house orange with a purple door. The first show he mounted, for neighborhood children sitting cross-legged on the shag carpet, was *The Seventh Princess*, Eleanor Farjeon's tale of a gypsy queen who shaves her youngest daughter's head so the girl can run away free, while six older daughters compete by hair-growth to earn the throne, in the end tending their equal-length locks forever.

Jane didn't want to be a shaved-head gypsy. She wanted long golden hair. She wanted a father like other fathers.

He belonged to Cora last, after *The Tonight Show* made him famous, Sharper Image merchandised his puppets, and his money attracted younger women like Cora's mother. Cora enjoyed orthodontia, a suite in a big house, private schools. While Jane saw his marionettes as rivals, to Cora they were beloved siblings. The frog prince, the soldier with his tinder-box, sisters who conversed in jewels or toads, father-kings who regretted in the end not loving their daughters enough.

On weekends, Cora and her father made puppets together, flour from papier-mâché crusting their fingernails.

Rosie, the middle daughter, couldn't claim him at all. The product of one night with a puppet show fan, she visited Jane's Ginkgo Street house when Walter remembered to invite her. She walked through the bodies hanging from the marionette bridge, feeling them swing against her face. Her favorite was the ugly duckling that, inside out, transformed into a swan.

꩜

WHILE WALTER NAPPED IN HIS NEW ROOM, HIS DAUGHTERS cleared out his suite in assisted living. A Bevins orderly dropped off packing boxes and a hand truck. "You ladies keep an eye on the weather. They're calling for ice." He left them to it.

Jane pulled a cardboard carton over to Walter's small desk. "I'll take his important papers to my house." She already had most of his documents: his Medicare card and checkbook, his long-term care policy, the power of attorney she needed to do his banking. She opened a leather portfolio that her father would never let her touch. "Here's his will."

"We shouldn't look at that," Rosie said.

"Why not?"

"It seems disrespectful. He's not dead yet."

"Well he's not competent to change it, so we might as well know what it says." Jane flipped through the legal-sized pages. The other two peeked over her shoulder despite themselves.

"'My Czech marionette collection to the Smithsonian,'" Jane read.

Cora nodded, approving.

"'To my daughter, Jane Nebel Gray, my gypsy princess marionette, to care for and preserve.'" Jane remembered the puppet from her father's favorite fairy tale. Butchered black hair under a red kerchief, mouth twisted in a perpetual acrylic smirk. "What am I supposed to do with it?"

She kept reading. "'To my daughter, Margo Rose (Rosie) Calhoun, my ugly duckling-swan marionette. To my daughter, Cora Baird Gray, the rest of my puppets, with hope that she will display them in the corporate offices of Gray Steed Puppets. To my daughters, all the rest and residue of my estate, in equal parts.'"

Rosie felt warm inside. She had never been sure he would treat her like the others. She teared up at being included.

Jane flipped through the will, to a page at the end where their father's pointy black pen strokes shouted from a codicil page. "'Conditions.'" She ran a thumbnail under each line as she read. "'The aforementioned gift and devise to my daughter, Jane, is contingent on her creating a puppet.'"

In reaction to her unstructured childhood, Jane had eschewed all things creative. She took pride in being practical. "No, thanks," she said.

Cora suppressed a smile.

"There's more," Jane said. "'The aforementioned gift and devise to my daughter, Cora, is contingent on her coming out from behind the stage to live among humans.'"

"Ridiculous," Cora murmured, losing the smile. She lived among humans. She ran his entire company, didn't she?

"What does it say about me?" Rosie asked.

"'The aforementioned gift and devise to my daughter, Rosie, is contingent on her not weighing more than two hundred pounds at the time of my death.'"

The sisters sat in silence. Humiliation sloughed off Rosie in hot waves. She had never been so embarrassed.

"When did he write that will?" Cora asked.

Jane checked. "The will, about ten years ago. This codicil four years ago. The fucker."

"I had forgotten how mean he could be," Cora said. "The dementia has made him nicer."

Rosie couldn't speak around the lump in her throat.

Jane searched the portfolio's other pockets. Stock certificates, life insurance policies, an envelope from a local lab. She looked at the page tucked inside. A paternity test, positive, a wide strip at the top torn off. Without a word she showed it to her sisters.

Rosie pressed knuckles to her mouth.

"Oh my God," Cora said.

Chapter 3

Once they knew of her, their missing sister hung in their minds like the last note of an unfinished scale.

Rosie imagined a sister the same weight as her, to the ounce. When they met, Rosie would know her sister's life story because it was her story, too, and that of every heavy girl. Her sister would have cultivated a light-footed way of moving, a smile, and good humor. She would know not to eat in front of others. She would take care with her makeup. Her clothing would not be stylish—above a certain size designers didn't manufacture cute clothes—but she would know how to accessorize. She would have a gold scarf around her neck, tied like a fashion model, in a manner that hid her chins. She would sport a purple leather purse that matched her purple top. Rosie herself tended toward beige, as camouflage, but if she had a sister to trade clothes with it might give her the courage to wear purple.

Never in her life had Rosie been able to share clothes with another person. The possibility infused her with happiness. She imagined herself with her new almost-twin, tête-à-tête, in an alliance that might almost withstand the combined power of Jane and Cora. Rosie's longing for this ally was so great she almost named her. "How will we find her?" she asked.

"Do we have to find her?" Jane said.

"Of course we do," Cora said.

Jane refolded the will. "Just what we need. A child to worry about."

"Who says she's a child?" Rosie said. "She could be a woman, older than you." In her mind, her well-appointed, confident twin aged just enough to pull rank on Jane.

Jane didn't accept that the sister could be older than her. Jane's mother, Ernestine, had told her Walter was a virgin when they met. Jane was sure it was a child, the product of a ridiculous and conceited old man too arrogant to use a condom. She was angry at her father for this. The mother of the girl would be Cora's mother, Luciana, all over again, another gold digger, only younger. Why couldn't men fall for women their own age?

Jane tried to wish the child away. "He could be conflating females. Mistaking Madison for his daughter instead of granddaughter. Or Kiki." She named Rosie's little girl and Rosie's prodigal mother, who had in the past demanded as much attention as a child.

"But the paternity test . . ." Rosie said.

Cora would welcome a little sister, would love to cede her role as the baby, but her thoughts were more abstract. Her father's projects were like his children. People thought her father had the magic touch, but he had experienced failures. One big disappointment was *Birdlandia*, a grandiose fantasy film he wanted to produce, dark and even sexual, cast entirely with puppets on a scale never seen before. Emboldened by Jim Henson's *The Dark Crystal*, her father had pitched it to Hollywood in the eighties, sure that his reputation would find him a studio, even though the puppeteering he envisioned was so physically demanding he would have had to recruit Olympic athletes. One planned scene required puppeteers to hang upside down from a scaffold like bats to animate magical flying creatures. The studio heads said no. Too dark, too expensive, too much liability. Children would have nightmares.

"It's not for children!" Walter had shouted to deaf ears.

That stillborn film was his baby. According to Cora's mother, he was depressed and angry for a year after the failure. "He would not be consoled," her mother always said dramatically when she told the story. "He didn't pull out of it until you were born."

Cora had seen the storyboard for the film in the Gray Steed archives, and its monstrous budget. The film wasn't feasible in 1985. But that was before computer-generated imagery. Today, with CGI, they could produce such a spectacle. Still, would it appeal? When she got back to New York she would search the archives and see.

"So what do you want to do?" Jane asked.

"We could place an ad," Rosie said.

"God no. We'd have every nut in the world claiming to be Dad's offspring." Jane imagined a long, straggly line of usurpers, and herself with a wooden staff, blocking each one. Too bad she couldn't hit people with sticks in real life. Still, it would be better to find and handle the sister now, not wait for a surprise.

"We could make them try on a glass slipper," said Cora, whose puppetry focused on fairy tales. "Or put a pea under their Sealy Posturepedics."

"So helpful," Jane said. She examined the paternity test. The date had been torn off but there was a patient number.

Rosie and Cora were looking at her expectantly. They would, of course, leave it to Jane to form a plan of action.

"I'll take it to the lab," she said. "If they have a record, that at least will tell us when he had it done."

They packed for another hour and loaded Walter's belongings on the hand truck. They wheeled it by their father's new room before they left, but he was sleeping, and only stirred and muttered when they told him goodbye.

Chapter 4

As a boy, Walter Gray learned marionettes from Mr. Svoboda. How the old man came to live in Raleigh, North Carolina, in 1952 was a mystery. Walter's parents felt sorry for him and sent Walter next door to offer Mr. Svoboda help with chores.

"I can do it myself, except one thing," Mr. Svoboda said. His living room smelled like stale saltines. "Come." He led Walter into the depths of the house. Walter wasn't afraid. Mr. Svoboda moved slow. Walter could outrun him.

In a back bedroom, puppets in various stages of completion covered the bed and dangled from a closet door. Fabric scraps draped a sewing machine. Mr. Svoboda picked up a small jar and shook eye screws onto an ironing board. "I can't feel my fingertips," he told Walter, his accent thick. His finger pushed the eye screws around like a clumsy broom but he couldn't pick them up.

Mr. Svoboda dragged a puppet body onto the ironing board. "First we decide where to put screws to fix strings. On hands, eye screw goes above space between fingers and thumb." Walter twisted in the screw. "Hands are linden wood—bass wood, you call it—from pallets. Is cheap and won't swell on the humid days. So many humid days you have here. I can't carve no more, but you can."

Walter placed the eye screws where Mr. Svoboda directed. The soldier puppet staring up at him seemed grateful. Mr.

Svoboda had him position the eye screws for the leg halfway between the knee and the bottom of the puppet's body. He handed Walter two pieces of wood fastened in a cross. "This we call a control, for controlling the puppet. Can be simple or fancy." He showed Walter another control that looked like an old-fashioned biplane. "My soldier needs this airplane control, so I can detach the extra leg bar, give him more movement."

With effort, he fastened strings between the puppet and the control.

"We use two strings for shoulders at center of control. Two strings from head to head-bar. One back string to balance, let him bend and straighten. When you put the head strings on, it throws off the balance, so you adjust the other strings."

Walter could see how the head and back strings formed a triangle, allowing the soldier to spin. Mr. Svoboda walked the puppet to test it, then had Walter move the screws on the legs a little lower.

"This puppet got a sword, so one more string for tip of sword."

"What about his nose?" Walter asked. The puppet had a large, bulbous nose that could support a string.

"Strings on nose will block the face, but sometimes for animals I put string on nose so they can look up."

Walter took in the room. Some of Mr. Svoboda's marionettes were old and expensive-looking, sculpted from wood, with beautiful paint and fur-trimmed clothing. "What do you do with these guys, anyway?"

"Used to be, I make the puppet show. First in parks and

fairgrounds, later for kings. Now, nobody want to see but I think of new puppets still and build them." Mr. Svoboda was getting winded. He sat down on the bed and wiped sweat from his forehead but didn't roll up the sleeves that were buttoned tight at his wrists. "Anyhow, you come after school, let me use your hands. You make puppet of your own and I teach you to dance it."

Chapter 5

The sisters pushed the hand truck through the Bevins Estate's automatic front doors, then stopped.

"Holy shit," Jane said. The parking lot was a skating rink. Ice beaded on power lines and bent tree limbs. Chips sheeted from the sky.

"There's no way you two can make it home in this," Cora said. "The house is close. Spend the night there." By "the house," she meant the six-thousand-square-foot luxury home she had grown up in. Their father still owned it, but now it served as accommodation for puppeteers visiting the Walter Gray Center for Puppetry at nearby North Carolina State University. Cora stayed there when she came to town and had it to herself this weekend.

Jane and Rosie didn't have a choice. Rosie called Gary to tell him to keep Madison overnight. They loaded boxes into Jane's Subaru and Jane drove white-knuckled to the MacArthur Downs gated community, where a blowing wintry mix obscured the golf course and neighboring brick mansions. MacArthur Downs had been developed in the eighties for the nouveau riche like Walter Gray who didn't quite feel welcome in Old Raleigh. Jane parked at the bottom of the drive. The sisters slipped and slid up the driveway to the house, Jane at one point crawling on all fours to keep from falling. Shards of ice covered the ground, tinkling as the women shuffled through. It was as if some giant had hurled a cut-glass bowl, shattering it into a billion pieces.

That evening, as the power flickered, the daughters sat at the kitchen table eating leftovers from the birthday party trays and drinking wine from a collection the management company maintained in the basement. They had everything they needed. The staff kept clean sheets on the beds and spare toothbrushes in the bathrooms.

"There it goes," Jane said as the power went off. She was prepared, with candles and the flashlight from her car. She lit the candles. Light wavered on her sisters' faces, shadows catching Rosie's bulk and the swish of Cora's high pony-tail. Cora's hair was the color of straw. Not the burnished gilt of straw spun into gold by small tyrants in fairy tales, but translucent, like hollow shafts of hay. Freckles bridged her small nose. She had the perfect hair for that high pony, sleek but not thin. And the perfect head, evenly shaped on a gazelle neck. Jane was taken with Cora's beauty but also jealous. Jane's hair was thick, especially now that it was gray under the brown dye. If she wrestled it into a ponytail holder, it stuck out in a bushy mass instead of hanging down.

Rosie took a candle and excused herself to use the bath-room.

Jane poured a fourth glass of wine from the house col-lection.

"Easy there," Cora said.

"What do you care? It's on Dad. This Chardonnay is much better than the shit I buy at Vonich for $2.99."

Cora dipped the tip of her pinky in candle wax and let it cool like a cap. She made the finger bow to Jane. "How about those will conditions? You could make a puppet. It wouldn't kill you."

"You could live among the humans."

Cora tossed her ponytail. "I live among the humans. I'm out in the world for Dad constantly."

"How's your boyfriend?" Jane asked. "What's his name? Rod?"

"We broke up," Cora said.

"Ah," Jane said, as if that proved something.

"We never had time to see each other." Cora didn't add that she never missed Rod when they were apart. Cora suspected that she didn't feel things with the emotion others felt. The men she dated either loved her more than she loved them and grew clingy, or they were like her: detached. *What if you found someone who cared for you exactly the same amount you cared for them?* She wondered what that would feel like.

"You make a puppet and I'll join humankind." Cora crooked her waxy pinky at Jane but Jane refused to pinky swear.

"Both highly unlikely," Jane said.

From the hallway, Rosie eavesdropped on her sisters. All Jane had to do was make one silly puppet, and their father's demand for Cora was too abstract to enforce. Only Rosie had a real condition to meet.

She coughed to let her sisters know she was there, and joined them at the table.

Jane sloshed more wine in her glass, licking a drop from her hand when it spilled.

"Let's play a game," she said.

Rosie groaned. Jane was famous for only playing games she knew she would win.

"We have to tell something we stole," Jane said. "You first, Rosie."

"Why Rosie? It's your big idea—you go first," Cora said.

"You don't mind, do you Rosie?" Jane said.

Rosie thought of food items she had pilfered as a child, Lifesavers from the candy rack at Vonich, a Twinkie from a classmate's lunch bag, but she was embarrassed to confess to those. "I stole Kaspar, from the Amahl puppets."

On Christmas Eve, the one holiday Rosie spent at Walter's house, Walter would put on a record album of Gian Carlo Menotti's children's opera *Amahl and the Night Visitors*. Rosie and Jane, and later Rosie and Cora, would act out the story of the three kings visiting the home of Amahl, a crippled shepherd boy, on their way to see the Christ child. The puppet stage was from the Jane years, a three-by-four piece of plywood framed with molding, out of which Walter had jigsawed a stage opening in the shape of a Middle Eastern minaret. Pencil lines still showed where he had sketched the spire. Walter designed the stage to hang from the ceiling at the foot of a staircase, so that more than one puppeteer could sit comfortably on the steps behind it. He used a dowel and brass hoop clips to string a red curtain behind the stage opening, to hide the puppeteers from the audience.

The Amahl characters were simple stick puppets, with Styrofoam balls or round fishing corks for heads, sequin eyes, and cotton hair, their robes squares of cloth made fancy with pinking shears. Jane had fashioned Amahl's crutch from Q-tips. Rosie liked to play Kaspar, the silly king, who traveled with a box of licorice. Walter had glued a silver box where Kaspar's hands should be.

"Why Kaspar?" asked Jane.

Rosie shrugged. She had felt, the Christmas of the theft, that it was the end of something, and she had been right. Jane was absent, spending the holiday with her new in-laws. Walter planned an extended stay in New York—Rosie had heard him and Cora's mother, Luciana, hissing at each other in the kitchen. The puppets themselves were disintegrating with age, old glue expiring and Styrofoam flaking. There wouldn't be any more Christmas Eve puppet shows.

The annual Amahl performance was one of the few times Rosie felt like part of the family. She stole the puppet as a memento of inclusion.

Cora's brow crinkled. "But I've seen that box of puppets within the last few years, and I'm sure Kaspar was in there."

"I put him back before I went home that night. The guilt was too much," Rosie said.

"That wasn't stealing. Those puppets were yours as much as ours," Cora said.

"I guess," Rosie said, but it hadn't felt that way.

Jane warbled an imitation of Amahl trying to convince his mother three kings had arrived at their door. "What about you, Cora? What have you stolen?"

Cora shook her head. "Nothing."

"Bullshit," Jane said.

"I'm serious. I've never stolen anything."

"Not even a lipstick from the drugstore? Every teenage girl does that," Jane said.

"If I wanted it, I bought it," said Cora, who had never lacked for anything.

"Surely you've stolen something." Jane could hear the slur in her own voice. "Someone's thunder. Someone's joy." She tossed back another swallow of wine. "Someone's birthright." Her sisters exchanged a look. Jane knew she was being obnoxious, but she couldn't help it.

Cora cleared her throat. "Your turn, Jane. What did you steal?"

When Jane started this game, she intended to tell a stock story about the malted milk balls she stole from Corston's Pharmacy when she was eight, how the package split open and the brown balls rolled down the drugstore's less-than-plumb floor all the way to the cashier's station. She had told that story many times. But now, she remembered another theft.

She was thirteen, in the art supply store at NC State that smelled of linseed oil and fumy inks. She'd saved money for a new sketchbook, but then, on the next shelf over, she saw the charcoal pencil set. It seemed to glow in a light of its own: pencils of every hardness, porous charcoal sticks, a blending stump and a kneadable eraser, soft as gum, to swallow dust. Jane could never afford it. She would die from the waiting before she could save enough babysitting money. What beauty she could capture if she had this set instead of her number two Ticonderogas.

Jane slipped the pencil set into the wide front pocket of her hooded sweatshirt. Blood pounded in her ears. She checked out with the sketchbook and left the store, closing her eyes as she passed through the entrance for fear an alarm would go off or store security would burst from the back and call for her to halt. But no one stopped her.

The Puppeteer's Daughters

At home, she took the pencils and sketchbook to the basement where her father was rehearsing his marionettes. He ignored her, deep in concentration. She lay on the floor in front of the marionette bridge. She preferred pencil as her medium because paint was too hard to control, her intentions foiled in the space between brush and canvas. With pencil, the contact was direct and she could make it do her bidding. Looking up, she liked the view of her father's triangular jawbone and the caverns of his nostrils, the way light from the overhead bulb sifted through his wild eyebrow hairs, his slight triumphant smile as he manipulated the puppets.

By suppertime the heel of her hand was shiny with charcoal dust. She was so absorbed she didn't hear her mother's heavy tread and startled when Ernestine came downstairs to announce dinner.

"In a minute," her father said, practicing again and again the swing and plant of his soldier puppet's booted foot.

Ernestine saw the pencils. "Where'd you get those?"

"Avril gave them to me as an early birthday present," Jane said, the lie coming to her with astonishing ease. Ernestine narrowed her eyes but didn't press it.

Jane had read "The Tell-Tale Heart." She knew that some people felt guilty after stealing and couldn't enjoy the thing they stole. That was not the case with her. She treasured those pencils. She sharpened them carefully so as not to waste a millimeter. In their honor, she made sure every line she drew was worthy. To this day she had a callus on her middle finger and one on her outside pinky from all the work she had created with that set.

Chapter 6

Cora and Rosie left Jane to finish her wine and carried flickering candles down the hall toward their bedrooms.

"I hope she's not too hungover in the morning," Rosie said.

"Serves her right." Cora squeezed Rosie's elbow. "It's like old times, us here together."

Rosie's face flushed. "Actually, I never spent a night in this house."

"You didn't?"

"My mamaw always came for me on Christmas Eve, and Dad drove me home when I babysat you, no matter how late they got back."

Cora guessed that her mother, Luciana, hadn't been keen on hosting Rosie overnight. Luciana wasn't known for her hospitality.

"Well, now's your chance. If you need anything let me know." Cora stopped at the door to her childhood bedroom.

Rosie peeked inside. "Your room looks different."

"Thank God, right?" Cora said. If it had still boasted the pink bedspread and posters of the Backstreet Boys her mother had foisted on Cora in middle school it would have been even harder to peck out of childhood roles. Instead of preserving it as a shrine to Cora, her father had the decorators come when she finished college, and now the room was neutral guest quarters. Best of all, there were no puppets in it. Puppets were Cora's life, but sometimes she needed a break. She imagined mothers of young children felt this way.

Cora said goodnight to Rosie and closed the bedroom door. She blew out the candle and got in bed. A few minutes later she heard Jane enter the shared bathroom, brush her teeth, and spit. She thought about Jane's birthright comment.

Cora didn't know what to do with Jane's resentment. If Cora could take off the heavy mantle of Gray Steed Puppets and gift it to Jane, she would, but Jane wouldn't want it.

When Cora was six, her father made the mistake of telling her about an orange kitten he'd seen scrounging around the McDonald's dumpster. Cora named the kitten Cupcake sight unseen and insisted he bring it home. The kitten did not fit his new name. Being abandoned so young had stunted his socialization. Used to living on whatever was smeared on thrown-out napkins, he would grab and hoard any balled-up piece of paper, growling at anyone who tried to take it away. Even after years of living in luxury with Cora's family, weighing in at twenty pounds, Cupcake still hissed if you tried to take his napkin. Jane was the same. Cora's therapist called it scarcity mentality, caused by deprivation during the formative years.

Their father had helped Jane financially as an adult. He paid the down payment on her condo when she divorced, but it was childhood money that mattered, apparently. What was Cora supposed to do with that? The divide between her and Jane seemed insurmountable.

The Puppeteer's Daughters

She remembered sitting on the back steps of the MacArthur Downs mansion with her father in summer, both of them barelegged and barefooted, the sleepy drone of a plane overhead and the scent of honeysuckle wafting from the golf course fence. Walter's gypsy princess marionette was scratching Cupcake's chin. The cat lay on his back, eyes closed, head lolling off the step while the puppet's wooden fingers raked furrows in his fur. Walter's movements were patient and meditative, as if there were no place else he needed to be. Dark hairs sprouted from his knuckles—from childhood, Cora had more clear memories of his hands than his face.

"You do it," he said. He kept the control but let her intercept the strings. She bent the gypsy's elbow and stroked Cupcake's jaw, half afraid the cat would rouse and bite her, but Cupcake purred on.

Lying in her childhood bed, Cora wondered, *What would be the equivalent of scratching Jane's chin?*

Chapter 7

In the king-sized guest bed, Rosie pulled soft sheets up to her chin.

For her, this mansion and the other places her sisters and father had lived were push-pins on a map. No more than five miles apart in west Raleigh and neighboring Cary were this house, Jane's childhood Ginkgo Street split-level, Jane's current condo, and Bevins nursing care. Even Jane's mother, Ernestine, had an apartment nearby. Their homes were like girls clustered on a playground, backs turned to Rosie, who lived twenty miles away in Deaverville, a small farm town where the train once stopped, that had so far resisted becoming one more Raleigh bedroom community. Rosie had inherited her house from her grandmother, who raised her. She supposed she would always live there.

She listened to wind hurl sleet against the window, the sound muted by the mansion's expensive double panes. So different from her own house, where night noises seeped through cracks. Pine cones dropping, the hoot of a barred owl, the train rumbling by a mile away.

Luciana hadn't let Rosie spend the night in the MacArthur Downs mansion, but Jane's mother, Ernestine, had been more welcoming. When Rosie was four and Jane was twelve, Rosie slept over for the first time at the Ginkgo Street house. Walter appointed Jane her host. Rather than share her room, Jane set up the sleepover in the basement, where Walter had his puppet stage.

"Do you want the couch or the air mattress?" Jane asked.

Rosie shrugged, just happy for the attention of a big sister. "The couch, I guess."

"All right. Excuse me." Jane went upstairs, closing the basement door behind her. Rosie heard her screaming at her parents: "She took the couch. *I* wanted the couch! She *always* gets the couch!"

"She's never slept here before!" Walter protested.

"I don't care!"

In a moment, Jane came back down, calm, as if nothing had happened.

"Jane, you can have the couch," Rosie offered, her heart beating hard in its cage.

"Oh, okay," Jane said.

Rosie had lain awake that night just like she was doing now. The Ginkgo Street basement was lit by a night-light and the passing headlights of cars. Behind the flipped-up curtains of the puppet stage, Walter's marionettes hung with their shadows. Magical by day, by night they were just this side of sinister. Rosie felt so lonesome, aware of Jane on the couch not wanting her there.

The next morning she had climbed the basement stairs in search of breakfast. Ernestine and a friend were having coffee in the kitchen. "You could leave him," the friend was saying. "Take the girl and go."

Now, outside, sleet turned to rain. Rosie stretched out her arms and legs. Her daughter, Madison, would love this king-size bed. She would want to jump on it, and Rosie would let her. One little old forty-pound girl wouldn't do any damage. As for safety, the bed was bigger than the trampoline in Rosie's yard. The mattress went on for miles, plenty of protection from falling. "Stay in the middle," she would tell Madison.

The imagined conversation made her miss Madison with a fierceness akin to physical pain.

Chapter 8

Cora woke early, to the sound of water dripping off gutters. She looked out. The temperature had risen during the night, reducing the ice to harmless slush. Vapor rose from the street. She dressed and found the keys to the red Mercedes SUV the management company kept for visiting puppeteers. She would buy a newspaper and coffee before her sisters woke up.

She drove to CVS, got her newspaper, and took her time browsing, not in a hurry to return to the house, where she and her sisters were bound to regress to their childhood roles: Jane in charge, Rosie to be pitied and not depended on, and Cora the privileged baby. Cora wished she could change the narrative, reinvent all of them. Why did they discount Rosie anyway? She couldn't think of a single bad decision by Rosie, unless you counted choosing Gary as her mate, though Cora could see what Rosie saw in Gary. He was fun, happy-go-lucky. Maybe they had imputed to Rosie the chaos her mother, Kiki, had wrought before she got sober, but how fair was that?

Cora could see a new narrative for Rosie, but how to rewrite Jane? Jane was writ in indelible ink.

In the toy aisle, Cora found blue rubber Zeno finger puppets and coloring books with Zeno and his friends waving from the cover. Alice was right that the toys, made in China, subsidized Gray Steed Puppets' more serious artistic work. After his big break with Zeno on Johnny Carson's show, Walter had focused on adult audiences to distinguish himself from Jim Henson, sensitive to critics calling his new foam creations "off-brand Muppets." But before long he was doing children's programming as well, even though he resented it, because that's where the money was.

The first day Cora interned at Gray Steed Puppets as a teenager, Walter threw her onto the set of *Zeno and Friends*. She remembered the flurry of colored fur and the scent of hot glue, booms looming overhead, a makeup artist powdering shine off a child actor's nose.

"Cora, over here. You're right-handing for Alf," her father called. She hopscotched between electrical cables taped to the floor.

Walter's old friend Alf Anderson held up a large peach-colored monster puppet with a bow in her hair. "Meet Peppy. Peppy is learning to share today."

"Stand behind Alf's shoulder. Slip your arm inside." Walter showed Cora how to operate the right hand while Alf did the left hand and mouth. Peppy was a live-hand puppet, with gloves at the end of the arms so she could pick up objects. "When Zeno asks for a lick of her lollipop, you grab it with Alf to keep Zeno from taking it."

"I'm thinking I make her voice a little gravelly? Not as sweet as when Stefan does Peppy?" Alf tried out a girl-monster voice. "That's *my* lollipop, Zeno!"

"Yeah, I like that." Walter slipped Zeno onto his own arm and yelled in falsetto, "You're such a hoarder, Peppy!" Then, in his own voice, "Places everybody! Let's get this in one take."

The Puppeteer's Daughters

Cora held her aching arm over her head, sweat running into her eyes from the heat of the lights. On the raised set, the little boy playing Zeno's human friend tried to explain to Peppy why she should share. "You hurt Zeno's feelings." He rested his cheek on Zeno's head. Cora could tell he half-believed Zeno was real, even though her father stood under Zeno making the puppet move. "Aww," said Zeno.

A trio of beetle puppets burst into a song about sharing, antennas waving. Peppy succumbed to guilt and shared her lollipop. Walter called "Cut!" and Cora pulled her tingling, sweaty arm free with relief.

Walter's vice president, Alice, stepped onto the set. She smiled at Cora. "How's your first day?"

"Good!" Cora watched fondly as Walter and Zeno shook the child actor's hand before the little boy's mother led him off set.

As soon as the child was out of earshot, Zeno yelled, "Hey, Peppy, I've got a lollipop you can suck!" Zeno started chasing Peppy around the studio.

"Dad!" Cora was shocked.

Alice laughed out loud. "I forgot to tell you. One of your jobs is to shout the code word 'bananas' when any kid comes on set."

"Okay," Cora said.

Walter chased Alf to the studio door, where they both collapsed, laughing. "It's about *sharing*, Peppy!" Zeno yelled.

"Welcome to Gray Steed Puppets," Alice said.

In those early days, Cora had done everything from wrangling body puppeteers, to sewing on feathers, to making props. Now it was all budgets and legal and human resources headaches. Her father's last will and testament demanded she get a life. She had a life, laboring for Gray Steed Puppets to preserve Walter's legacy and establish her own. The lengths she had to go to in order to claim time for herself behind a puppet stage—getting up at five every morning, forswearing time wasters that she might otherwise have enjoyed: TV, social media. Friends. All so that she could get back to her puppet creations on a regular basis and not forget what she had already invented.

She wiggled a rubber Zeno on her pinky and made it speak in a sarcastic whisper. "Live among the humans, Cora!"

A CVS worker walking down the aisle smiled. "He's from here, you know. Walter Gray."

"Yes, I know." Cora put the puppet back.

She wandered to the cosmetics aisle and ran her fingers along the tubes of lipstick: Pink Passion, Sassy Mauve. Rose Red.

Every teenage girl does that.

Fairy tales were fraught with thievery. Giants reported missing golden harps, bears filed insurance claims for stolen porridge, soldiers scammed old women out of tinderboxes.

Cora palmed a lipstick and slipped it into her pocket.

Chapter 9

The power came on with a hum around nine o'clock, the click and blink of the digital clock by the bed waking Rosie up. She padded to the kitchen and found pancake mix in the cabinet, and a jar of crystallized honey that she set in warm water on the stove to reconstitute. She picked out blueberries from the fruit salad left over from Walter's birthday party to add to the pancakes.

Cora came in from outside, carrying a newspaper and a cardboard drink holder with three large coffees. "What are you doing?"

Rosie didn't want Cora to think she was scrounging food for herself. "Figuring out our breakfast."

"Great." Cora gave Rosie one of the coffees. The empty wine bottles from last night still crowded the table. Cora put them in the recycle bin.

"Can't believe we drank all that," Rosie said, spraying the last of a can of nonstick cooking spray in a skillet.

"Blame Jane," Cora said. She sat at the table with her knees up, sipping coffee while Rosie cooked. "How do you feel about a new sister?"

"I hope there is one," Rosie said. "I want to find her."

"Me too. If she exists. He didn't mention a fourth daughter in his will." She snorted. "Can you believe that will?"

The hurt from yesterday came back. Rosie's eyes stung. She was glad Cora couldn't see her face.

"He wants Jane to make a puppet," Cora said. "That'll be the day. I've never seen her create anything. Even when her boys were little, it was always Pete doing arts and crafts or music with them, never Jane."

"She used to draw." Rosie tested the skillet with a drop of batter. "She was good." She remembered Jane sketching a girl with braids that looked three-dimensional, how Jane left a little dot of white in the eyeballs to bring them to life. Rosie poured the first circle of berry-filled batter in the pan, let it bubble and brown, flipped it. "Jane's more likely to make a puppet than I am to lose weight."

"You don't have to lose weight, Rosie. There has to be another way for you to get your share."

It was a new sensation for Rosie to have a sister take her side. It felt nice, but Jane was executor, not Cora.

As she cooked, Rosie thought about what Walter's money could buy for her and Madison. Madison could go to college, a good college, something Rosie had not done. She pictured Madison in a cap and gown, all grown up, walking across a stage to claim her diploma. She imagined herself in the audience, cheering, except the Rosie she imagined was thin, having lost a hundred pounds.

She stacked pancakes on a plate and put them and the honey on the table. "You and Jane can split these."

"Aren't you going to have some? God, they smell good. You're a magician, conjuring these from nothing."

"You go ahead. I'll stick with fruit salad." Rosie's stomach growled.

Jane came in, wearing one of the Egyptian cotton bathrobes the management company provided. She checked a text on her phone. "Bevins. Dad had a good night." She sat down at the table. "Probably doesn't even remember his old room."

Cora took a lipstick from her pocket and offered it to Jane. "Do you want this? It's more your shade than mine."

"Sure," Jane said, looking pleased. She twisted the lipstick and tried it on. "A robe *and* a free lipstick. I could get used to this place."

Chapter 10

W e hang hands lifted up," Mr. Svoboda always said.
No puppet's hands ever drooped to its sides at rest.
Sometimes Walter felt like a marionette himself. Before every show he ever gave, whether in his basement or Carnegie
Hall or on *The Late Show*, he addressed the audience with
his hands cupped in offering as if lifted by invisible strings.
Here. Here is what I have for you.

He apprenticed with Mr. Svoboda through high school
and college. They entertained at children's birthday parties
and Walter got a five-minute spot on the local television
news, his meteorologist puppet a foil to the real weatherman. At NC State, Walter met another puppeteer, Ernestine. He was in bed with Ernestine when he got the call that
Mr. Svoboda was in the hospital.

Mr. Svoboda looked small in the bed. In the short-sleeved hospital gown his arms were uncovered, and
Walter saw for the first time the blue-stenciled number
on his forearm. Mr. Svoboda's grip when Walter took his
hand was surprisingly strong, even painful. He died in
the night.

Walter took Ernestine to Mr. Svoboda's house. In those
days, Ernestine wore her yellow puppet, Tino, on her left
hand as an accessory, making him talk to strangers and tickle
children with his crazy rainbow hair. In those days, Walter
found it charming.

He used the key Mr. Svoboda kept hidden in an old gardening glove and led Ernestine to the back room.

"Ooooh, is dark and scawwy in here," Tino said.

One by one, Walter hauled out the cast he and Mr. Svoboda had created together. He found the soldier he had strung the day they met, and the first puppet he had made without Mr. Svoboda's help, a gypsy princess with a tiny red kerchief hiding her scissored hair. In the dozens he laid out on Mr. Svoboda's ironing board, he could see his handiwork evolve from clumsy to refined and imagined hearing Mr. Svoboda's instructions:

"On main control, your right index finger hold most of the weight. The left hand work the arms and legs."

"Don't restrict with the costume. The best manipulation no good if puppet can't move inside his clothes."

"Let audience see the character thinking."

"Audience must believe your character is alive."

Walter's art had moved beyond Mr. Svoboda's. Nine strings became eleven and he improved the airplane controls. He switched to black braided Dacron line that didn't reflect light on stage. Mr. Svoboda used to say, "The mirror is your friend. You see a movement or position you like, look down with the bird's eye and memorize it." Since starting at the TV station, Walter had instead learned to use a monitor to frame his marionettes so he could see what the audience saw at home.

"Ooooh," Tino said, helping Ernestine open a box. "What's these?" Inside were the antique marionettes Mr. Svoboda had smuggled out of his homeland. A knight on a gray horse, a harlequin, a Punch and Judy with crescent-moon profiles, beaked noses bowing to meet curved chins.

"These must be worth a fortune," Ernestine said.

Walter cradled Punch—Pulcinella—holding the small body to his nose. In the dry must of old wood and brocade he smelled armies marching across a continent, ghostly footprints crossing each other in different centuries.

"Nice man not have a family . . ." Tino's words hung in the air for Walter to consider.

In the hospital, Mr. Svoboda hadn't been able to speak, but Walter imagined the words he would have rasped if he could: "I give you my puppets. I want you to have them."

Walter and Ernestine packed all the puppets and loaded them into Walter's Volkswagen camper.

Chapter 11

In fairy tales, mothers are always dead. That wasn't the case for Jane, Rosie, and Cora. The girls' three mothers were very much alive.

On Monday, Jane called her mother, Ernestine. "Besides Rosie, do you think Dad had any other love children?"

"Not on my shift," Ernestine said. Then, suspicious, "Why?"

"He said something at his birthday party about a fourth daughter."

"The bastard. There better not be a fourth. Don't let him screw you the way he screwed me."

In an epic lawsuit that had dragged on through Jane's twenties, Ernestine claimed that the Zeno character who made Walter famous was a knockoff of her own puppet character, Tino. Jane's parents had finally settled out of court for a sum that had barely satisfied Ernestine when paid, and lost half its value in the last market crash.

"You should get a third of his estate, not a fourth," Ernestine said. "All those years we had nothing, having to sew your clothes, couldn't scrape up field-trip money. Me working crap jobs to support his 'art' when he could have sold just one of those Czech marionettes to support us. Then he hits it big and raises Cora like a princess. He owes you."

"At least he didn't name a fourth daughter in his will," Jane said. She didn't want to share with another sister. But she needed to get this situation under control.

Jane worked for a property management company. Years of extracting rent from tenants had taught her that people found it harder to say no in person than on the phone. She stopped in at the lab that had tested her father's DNA, ignoring two shifty men in the lobby waiting to pee in cups. She showed her power of attorney to the young woman at the window. "I need to request my father's medical records."

The woman examined the document, its official date stamp from the Register of Deeds, the embossed notary seal. She handed Jane a release to sign. "It can take up to thirty days. We don't process records on site."

"That's fine," Jane said. She walked outside, where the sun had dried up all traces of the weekend's storm. Her phone dinged with her sisters' group chat. Rosie wished Cora a safe flight back to New York. Cora texted a photo for Rosie to show Madison, of birds nesting in the airport lobby and bathing in the water fountain.

Jane couldn't think of anything to text that wouldn't feel like an intrusion.

Chapter 12

Back in New York, Cora resumed her twelve-hour days at Gray Steed Puppets, until Friday arrived and she and her vice president, Alice, met for their Friday Sunset.

Alice was a dozen years older than Cora. She had joined Gray Steed right out of business school. When Cora started full-time at Gray Steed after college, Alice was the only other woman, as well as the only Black employee. At the first staff meeting, when Walter and the other male puppeteers oozed testosterone and Alf Anderson mansplained to Cora the importance of theme in puppet shows, Alice caught Cora's eye and a look of understanding passed between them. At the time, Gray Steed had outgrown its space and Alice was scouting new offices. Alice took Cora along to look at the space she'd found, in a high-rise near the Flatiron Building, timing the visit for sunset. She walked Cora into the west conference room, where sun traced the Manhattan skyline in gold and pink filigree. "Look. This is for us." Gray Steed took the lease, and Alice and Cora started meeting on Fridays for end-of-day cocktails.

In those early years, Friday Sunset was their time to shut out the nerdy maleness of the place. To recount the most outrageous things the guys had done that week, and for Cora to get Alice's feedback on new performances. Alice would make their drinks and Cora would perform the latest in her *Tangled Tales* series.

Later, after Walter retired and Cora took over Gray Steed, she and Alice added long-term strategy to the Friday Sunsets. They didn't admit the men. They did sometimes admit other women—there were some now, a few female puppeteers and occasional interns. One young male puppeteer whined, "the two most powerful people in the company excluding people based on gender. We don't have the same access."

"Oh, boo hoo," Alice said. "Two thousand years of male supremacy in the business world, men dominating this company, and you're complaining about women networking for two hours a week over a gin and tonic. Give me a break. Get your own clubhouse."

Alice liked for Cora to perform before they talked business. Cora's *Tangled Tales* were short, no more than seven minutes. "They clear my head," Alice said.

Cora wasn't the first to change up a traditional fairy tale, but she was proud of her twists and her innovative puppetry. She had started with rod puppets but in the last year had moved the controls inside the clothed bodies. Her pieces looked like hand puppets, but internal rings and cords gave them a thousand nuanced gestures. Manipulating the rings like supple brass knuckles, Cora could eradicate the distance between the words she spoke in voice-over and the movement of the creature at the end of her hand. The words didn't merely inform the movement. Each word *was* a movement, and each movement a word, bringing her close to the perfect merge of language and kinesis. She knew she could never achieve it completely, but the striving created beauty.

The Puppeteer's Daughters

The *Tangled Tales* weren't Gray Steed property. Cora created them for herself and Alice alone, enjoying the technical challenge of developing the puppets' physicality to serve the story.

Years ago, when she was fresh out of college and had just joined Gray Steed, she had proposed a television pilot to Walter featuring her *Tangled Tales*. She expected him to say yes—he always said yes to her—but this time he shook his head. "Not viable."

"How do you know? I think they're really good."

He pinched the bridge of his nose wearily. "Your tales are beautiful, Cora. Don't stop making them, but don't expect to sell them. Swine don't appreciate pearls. You'll just be disappointed."

She defied him and set up meetings with TV executives herself.

In fairy tales, things happen in threes. In life, things happened in fours or fives or sevens, and sometimes not at all. Cora pitched her *Tangled Tales* to executives at every network. She got no takers. To a man—and they were all men—each executive asked her, "What does your father think about this?"

"I told you," Walter said when she reported back. "Developmentally appropriate children's curriculum pays the bills, not fairy tales." And yet Cora knew her dad loved fairy tales best of all. When she was small, it was fairy tales they would perform together on Cora's playroom stage, with his old marionettes. He refused to bring Zeno or his other foam puppets home.

The Friday Sunset conference room had a small whiteboard that she used as her stage. As Cora set up, she ran by Alice the idea of resurrecting Walter's film, *Birdlandia*.

"It could work," Alice said. "He was always ahead of his time. Mind you, CG isn't cheap." She narrowed her eyes at Cora.

"What?" Cora said.

"I just want to be sure your motives are sound," Alice said. "To make us money, not to impress Daddy. Daddy issues have no place in business."

"My daddy is unfortunately beyond impressing," Cora said.

Alice reached out and squeezed Cora's hand. The sun set like molten gold, reflected in every window.

"Let me make some calls, work up a budget." Alice poured a splash more gin in her drink. "What do you have for me today?"

"I recreated Dad's six princesses, minus the strings." Cora slipped the puppet on her hand. Her father's marionette had featured six identical princesses in one, able to bow in unison at the waist, golden hair sweeping the ground. She was pleased with her replica, six faces carved from poplar, features painted in acrylic with superglue over the eyes and lips for gloss.

In the original story of *The Seventh Princess*, a gypsy gives up her freedom to marry a king. She bears him six daughters who are fair like the king, and a seventh whose coloring is dark like her own. When she knows she's dying and asks the king which princess will succeed her, he decides the throne will go to the daughter whose hair is longest. Nurses take over the care of six princesses' hair, but the queen herself takes charge of the youngest, hiding her head with a red scarf. When the gypsy queen dies, the king measures his daughters' hair. The six golden-haired princesses tie. The seventh princess removes her scarf to reveal that her mother has snipped her dark hair short, freeing her to leave and seek adventure.

When Walter performed the tale for Cora with his marionettes, he always made the shaved-head gypsy princess leap and bound with joy as she ran away.

Cora readied the leather skull caps that would allow her to change out the six princesses' blonde wigs. "It's the sisters in middle age," she told Alice.

As the identical golden-haired princesses grew older, they differentiated. Some aged better than others. Hair thinned, some snuck off to have work done, others couldn't bring themselves to spend the money. Some gained weight, causing physical discomfort on the dance line.

The gypsy princess hadn't written home in years. The last word her six golden-haired sisters had of her came from the servant who had run away with her, when he returned to the kingdom to retire near family. "She's well," he reported. "In summer she runs a market stall in Blandenburg, homemade goat's milk soaps and cheeses. In winter she travels—I don't know where, but she returns tanned and refreshed."

"Ah," the golden-haired princesses said politely. Their memories of their gypsy sister had faded. Sometimes they thought of her on their laps when she was small, her olive skin darker than theirs, the kerchief always on her head per their mother's orders. Even then she had smelled wild, of fresh air or the sky before a snow.

Their father died, and the gypsy princess didn't come, though she sent flowers: wild asters still bearing the dirt of some far-off hillside. Her note addressed her sisters by name, she alone remembering the six names they themselves had long forgotten: Andrea, Betina, Chantalle, Davina, Evelyn, and Fatima.

Reading the note as the other sisters combed out their hair after the funeral, one sister asserted her wish to be called by name instead of generically "princess."

"What is your name?" another sister asked. In truth, the first could not remember, but she picked one from the list. "Betina," she said with authority.

"Betina," her sisters practiced in unison.

"Check this out," Cora said to Alice. Unlike her father's prototype, her six sisters were detachable, fitted together with pegs, so they could physically break apart. She disconnected Betina from the others.

"This isn't bad," Betina said, stretching stiff joints, enjoying the room to move. "This isn't bad at all."

"Ahh," the princesses said when Betina broke away. A strange feeling ran through them, not painless but a satisfying kind of pain, like the picking off of a lingering scab when the wound underneath has healed.

"That metaphor is a little gross," Alice said.

"I'm going to find our sister," Betina said. Somehow she knew she would find her, even though Betina had never left the palace walls and there was no return address on the gypsy sister's note.

When Betina left, there was silence for a moment. Hair brushes paused.

"I've been thinking," said one princess, "that I might cut my hair short, shorter, you know, frame my face, some feathering."

"Us too?" asked all her sisters immediately.

"Well no," she said, "just me."

"That's as far as I've gotten," Cora said.

Someone knocked on the conference room door.

"Occupied!" Alice called.

"Any suggestions?" Cora said.

"On the servant, I hear the mechanism," Alice said. "Like dentures clicking."

"Annoying, huh?" Cora turned the servant inside out. She used this androgynous puppet for multiple roles— servant, crone, suitor, whatever a story called for. She had rigged five metal rings, one for each finger, connected with piano wire to points inside the puppet. Working the piece was complicated. No one else would be able to manipulate it like she did.

"Quite a contraption," Alice said.

"I'm experimenting. It's working, but if the rings were fitted, and lighter, they might be quieter."

"Alf has a custom machinist he uses sometimes. I'll get you the name." Alice swirled ice in her glass. "Interesting, the search for the sister. Where did that idea come from?"

Cora could have confided in Alice about the paternity test. Alice could guard a secret. But she decided to keep it to herself until they knew more. She turned the servant puppet right side out. "I guess seeing Jane and Rosie got me thinking about sisters."

Chapter 13

Some guys are princes, some are frogs.

Rosie enjoyed sex in the daytime. It made her feel like she was getting away with something. And she was. Gary had laid his cell phone on the nightstand, on vibrate. Every few minutes it buzzed as his current girlfriend, Amber, got madder and madder looking for him.

He had come by to help Rosie fix the lid on Madison's toy box so it wouldn't fall down and crush her fingers, and they'd wound up in bed. Now he leaned against the headboard with his eyes closed, his arm around Rosie's shoulder, trailing a tickling finger along her upper arm. He was naked except for the bedspread he'd pulled over one leg.

Everything about Gary was long and lean, from the raised veins in his arms to the pointy dark goatee on his chin. His fingers were a knuckle longer than Rosie's when they pressed their palms together, not that they pressed their palms together much anymore. These days when Gary came over it was all wham-bam, thank-you-ma'am. In the light that streamed through Rosie's bedroom window she could map all the familiar landmarks on his skin—the tattoo of their initials he'd poked into his bicep with blue ballpoint ink when he and Rosie were in the tenth grade, the little hanging mole just under his left nipple. The trail of dark hair that led down to his half-awake penis. All things she missed when she didn't get to see him. Especially that last one.

She had to get up and dressed—her appointment at the weight loss clinic was in half an hour—but she didn't want Gary to leave. She never realized she was lonely until she had him back for a little while.

She swung her legs off the bed and reached for her bra.

Gary grabbed her hand. "Don't go, baby."

"I have to get a move on. I'm late."

"How long you going to be gone?"

"A couple hours, max. In time to pick up Madison at kindergarten."

She struggled to hook the clasp of her bra. Gary reached over and did it for her. "I'll stay and finish that toy box. Then take me a nap. Maybe we can do it again when you get back." His hands slid down her back and around her middle, sending a tingle across her skin. His breath puffed warm on her neck. "What kind of appointment you going to?"

She touched a scar on the knuckle of Gary's index finger that she hadn't noticed before. It felt so nice sitting here with his arms around her, like old times. "Just a physical," she lied. Gary wouldn't want her to lose weight. He liked a "handful" when he touched a woman, he said. He didn't care for bony women, though Amber was bony. "She ain't half the woman you are," he'd told Rosie.

He gave her breasts a squeeze then let her go so she could finish getting dressed. As she left the room his cell phone buzzed again. Rosie shut the door fast so she didn't have to hear him answer it.

The Puppeteer's Daughters

CHAIRS WERE THE FIRST THING ROSIE NOTICED WHEN SHE walked into the gastric bypass orientation. She was used to assessing the seating wherever she went, to see if she could actually expect to sit and rest instead of pretending she preferred to stand. The bariatric clinic's chairs were twice as wide as regular reception chairs. They were love seats almost, sturdy and easy to get out of without the spindly tapered legs so many doctors' offices seemed to favor. Plenty of space between them too. She guessed it made sense that the clinic would have chairs like that, since most of the people visiting were of the larger persuasion. She counted seven of those people in the audience now, five women and two men, potential patients like her thinking about having the surgery. Some had brought their normal-sized spouses with them. In terms of weight Rosie fell in the middle of the pack.

She took a seat in the back. A woman in a white lab coat who most definitely did not have a weight problem adjusted the mic at the front of the room. "Let's go ahead and start. Did everyone get the questionnaire we sent you? Tear off the first page with your contact information and hand that up to me now. We'll collect the rest later."

Rosie tugged the questionnaire out of her handbag. The eight pages had taken her all week to fill out—medical history, psychological history, description of past weight-loss efforts.

The girl next to Rosie leaned over and whispered. "I needed an extra sheet of paper to list all my diets."

"Have you tried a lot of different ones?" Rosie asked.

"You name it. South Beach, Nutrisystem, Weight Watchers, Jenny Craig, keto, Whole 30, grapefruit, high carb, low carb, no carb, one where I could only eat dinner between seven and eight at night—I either fit it in then or had to wait for breakfast." The girl pulled a lipstick from her shiny yellow handbag and deftly applied it without a mirror. She looked to be about Rosie's age, with similar light brown hair thinning on top, and blue eyes a shade lighter than Rosie's.

"Are you from around here?" Rosie asked. "I mean, were you born here?"

"Me? No. Germany. My daddy was in the Army."

Rosie felt silly. She couldn't go around wishing every overweight girl was her sister. She tore the page off her questionnaire and passed it to the front.

The woman in the lab coat introduced herself as Dr. Helen Hines, the clinic director, and dimmed the lights for a PowerPoint presentation. She went over what the doctor did during gastric bypass surgery, creating a small pocket of a stomach. She showed before and after photos of thin, smiling people happy with the results of their surgeries. She talked about all the ills the procedure could cure—diabetes, heart disease, creaky knees—none of which Rosie had, at least not yet. Finally at the end, Dr. Hines started listing all the things that could go wrong. Fluid leaking from the gastrointestinal tract into the abdominal cavity, causing infection or an abscess. Scar tissue making the opening to the pouch so small not even liquids could pass through. You had to have more surgery then, or starve. Something called "dumping syndrome," which sounded awful. Whenever you ate something with sugar in it your heart raced, you broke into a cold sweat and felt like you were falling, all for a good half hour or more. When Dr. Hines wrapped up by adding "death" to her list of bad outcomes, Rosie looked around to see if that bothered other people as much as it did her, but nobody seemed upset. Dr. Hines turned the lights back on.

"Rather than answer your questions here in the general session, we've arranged for each of you to meet individually with a nutritional counselor who will be able to address any concerns you have. Come up when I call your name, please."

The girl next to Rosie gathered her things. "I am so ready for this."

Rosie wished she could say the same. Right now she was fat but healthy. She didn't want to trade healthy for skinny. Dr. Hines called her name.

"Good luck!" her neighbor said.

"Thanks." Rosie walked up to where Dr. Hines waited with a young man holding a clipboard. "This is Nelson Davenport. He'll be your counselor if you decide to proceed with our program. He'll take you back to weigh in and talk to you about our process." Dr. Hines shook Rosie's hand with her own little bony one and called the next name.

Nelson took her forms. "This way, please."

She followed him down a short hall and looked away as she stepped on the scales. She had a general idea of what she weighed and didn't want to know if she'd gained any pounds. After he measured her height, Nelson wrote on his clipboard and led her to his office, which was very clean and didn't have a single personal item in it. Maybe he had to share it with other people. He sat down at the desk. Rosie made herself comfortable in the chair across from him. It wasn't as roomy as the chair in the orientation, but seemed sturdy enough that she didn't have to worry about breaking it.

Nelson paged through her paperwork. He looked tired, and not thrilled to be talking to her. She could tell he didn't really see her. She was just another faceless fat person to him. There he was, young and fit, probably went to the gym every day and ate right all the time. Maybe it even disgusted him that she'd let her weight get so out of control. That was okay. Lots of people wrote her off at first because of her size, but she'd win him over. She grew on people, her mamaw used to say. Sometimes she could pinpoint the very minute somebody who hadn't given her the time of day suddenly realized she was there in the room and halfway interesting. It might be a person she'd been introduced to two or three times, and always before when the friend introducing them said, "Rick, have you met Rosie?" Rick would say "no" at the same time as Rosie said "yes," which could be embarrassing. But then eventually the person would notice her. She'd see that spark of interest in their eye. And it wasn't just men and sexual interest, either. It was other human beings actually looking at her and seeing her instead of treating her like she was invisible or in the way. One of these days Nelson Davenport would look her in the eye and actually see Rosie Calhoun.

She knew how to be patient.

Only once in a while would a person appreciate her from the outset. Like Gary. The very first week of tenth-grade homeroom he'd asked her to the football game, then got his brother to take them to the Dairy Queen and cruising on Patterson Avenue. Of course she was prettier then, and people called her plump or maybe fat, but not obese like now. *Obese* was such an unforgiving word. *Morbidly obese.* Sounded like you were about to die. She'd watched a reality TV show last week where folks everybody used to call "midgets" or "dwarves" made clear those names weren't allowed anymore. They wanted to be called "little people." Well, maybe the obese of the world ought to insist on being called "big people" instead.

Gary hadn't broken up with her because she turned into a big person. He'd left because he couldn't handle those early weeks after Madison was born—the crying and the diapers that seemed like they'd go on forever. Fatherhood was just too much for him. And really it had been a relief when he called it quits and moved out. She could concentrate on Madison instead of worrying whether Gary was happy. He still came by, and he became a pretty good daddy once he'd had some practice. He dated other girls but never seemed serious about any of them, even Amber, who he'd been seeing for a while now. He and Rosie might not be together officially, but Rosie felt like she and Madison had his heart.

Nelson typed something into his computer. "We'll need a referral from your family doctor, and your insurance card so we can ask your insurance company to pre-certify you."

She handed him her card.

Nelson clicked the mouse, still looking at his screen. "You'll have to lose some weight before the surgery. What lifestyle changes have you made so far?"

"Hmm?" She wasn't sure what he meant.

"Are you exercising? Limiting your calories?"

"Well, no, not yet. I thought that started after the operation."

"No, it starts before. Based on your body mass index we'd like you to lose forty pounds to start with, to show you're motivated and to get to a weight that will make the procedure less risky."

"You mean I have to lose weight so I can have weight-loss surgery?"

"Yes."

"Nelson, honey, if I could lose weight I wouldn't need the gastric bypass."

"It's only forty pounds."

"It might as well be a hundred and forty. I've never been able to lose weight. Not even a pound. If I try to diet it just makes me think about food more and I get fleshier."

Nelson leaned back in his chair. "It's important to start now to get used to the food restrictions you'll have to follow after the surgery."

"No sugar, I know," she said.

"And no fat," he said.

"What kind of fat are we talking?"

"No red meat. No sauces. No gravy. No mayonnaise. No butter or margarine."

Rosie stared at him. It was like he had opened the refrigerator at her house and listed everything inside. "I can never have those anymore? Ever?"

"If you try to eat that type of food after surgery it'll make you sick." For a moment his face looked a little kinder. "Surgery's a big step. Are you sure it's what you want?"

She thought about the question.

It wasn't only about Walter's money, though Gary would say, "When people say it ain't the money, it's the money, honey." The money would be nice, but she could find a way to send Madison to college without it.

It was about being included. That moment when Jane read the will, before she read the conditions, was a moment more delicious than any food Rosie had ever let drip down her throat, and she wanted more.

She would overlook Walter giving her a harder condition than her sisters. It wasn't fair, and Walter was an ass, but Rosie would do it. Her sisters would have to move over and make room for her.

"I need to lose the weight," she said.

"Then let's see if we can change your eating habits. I'll personalize a food plan. Nothing too stringent. Think of it as a first step. You can use our FoodTracker app to record what you eat and look up the calories and fat content. Enter every bite, starting tonight—it's important to be honest. We'll meet back here in a week to see how it's going. How's that sound?" Nelson scribbled an appointment time on a business card.

Rosie chewed her lip. She had a long, loving relationship with food and she didn't want to give it up, any of it. But this was important.

"Okay," she said.

Chapter 14

F airy tales end with marriage to the prince. In real life, marriage continues, the prince and princess age, begin to grate on each other's nerves, sometimes commit offenses that cannot be forgiven.

Jane's phone showed a missed call from her ex-husband, Pete.

The same things that made Pete a great dad made him a poor husband. He related to their boys like he was one of them, down on the floor with their train sets, playing music with them in the garage. She married him because he made her laugh, something she sometimes forgot to do. Three events caused her to end it. First, he lost his job with a public relations firm and didn't tell her. Second, when she found out and confronted him, he blamed her for his failure to disclose, implying that he was scared of her. Third, she found him smoking pot in the garage with their sons. Jane didn't have a problem with Pete smoking weed as long as he spent his own money. But it was not acceptable to smoke it with your teenagers. Smoking with your children was like wearing curlers to Walmart. It meant you had given up, had let the last standard fall and were sliding down that slippery slope. It was the final straw.

The triple sins occurred during a three-month period. After the divorce, Jane had moments when she thought those three months were just a bad patch and she should have stuck it out, supported Pete through his midlife crisis. She certainly hadn't been happy post-divorce. But if she had stayed married, what would she and Pete be doing now? Their sons Neal and Brett were out of the house, still in need of shepherding but never coming home again. She and Pete could parent them without being a couple. So what would they do together? Pete had hobbies: his music, his beer-making, his woodworking. Between her job and managing Walter's care, Jane didn't have time for hobbies. She and Pete had nothing in common. She might as well be alone.

When Pete answered his phone she could hear guitar strains in the background. Brett must be jamming with Pete. She imagined the two of them, Brett with his clean-cut good looks, Pete with that ridiculous gray ponytail she wished she could chop off.

"You called?" she said.

"Yeah." The music stopped. "Hey, I have to tell you something you aren't gonna like."

Great, Jane thought.

"Brett's leaving school."

"No, he isn't," she said.

"He is. He got a chance to play with the Addled Pigs." Pete said the name of the band as if she should recognize it. "They're touring the southeast this spring so he's going with them."

"He's in his last semester of college." There was no way Brett was quitting now.

"It's a great opportunity for him," Pete said. "The Addled Pigs almost got an offer from Columbia Records last year."

"Almost?"

"He can finish school later."

"But he won't!" Brett would lose his momentum, Pete must know that. "He needs to graduate—then he can do what he wants."

"He can't let this pass him by." Pete's voice was wistful. He was living his own failed rock-and-roll fantasy through Brett.

"You're telling me the same dive bars won't still be there in four months?" She heard a guitar string twang in the background. "He's there with you? Put him on the phone."

With a sigh, Pete handed off the phone.

"Hi, Mom," Brett said warily.

"Are you out of your mind?"

"I want to play music."

"So play music—on your days off from a job that will support you." She'd been sending him job notices from Monster.com for the past six months.

"I'll make enough from the music."

"For beans and rice, maybe. What about health insurance?"

"I won't get sick. Please can we not have this conversation?"

She heard Pete say, "Let me talk to her again." He got back on the line. "I know you're upset, but we have to let him live his dream."

"No, we don't."

"It's hard for you to relate, not being an artist yourself, but we can't squelch his creativity. It'll kill him."

"Oh, shut *up*, Pete."

He was so patronizing, acting superior to her because he played a mediocre electric bass and could hit a note four times out of five. She hung up on him.

Jane knew what it was to be creative. She remembered the thrill when Ernestine brought home a new box of crayons, or cloth scraps Jane could use to make curtains and pillows for her dollhouse. The Ginkgo Street house overflowed with art supplies. Jane was always the best artist in her grade.

In eighth grade she won a statewide Scholastic Gold Key award for her drawing of Walter rehearsing his marionettes. The awards ceremony was at the North Carolina Museum of Art. She and the other winners from her school rode to the museum with their art teacher, Mr. Williams. Walter was to meet her there because Ernestine was out of town. The other winners' parents came. Jane kept watching the door, waiting for Walter. "I'll tell the judges to call your name last," Mr. Williams said, to give Walter time to get there. He never arrived.

When she got home, she found him in the sewing room, replacing a broken yoke string on his gypsy princess puppet.

"Where were you?" she demanded. If he had offered a good reason, a sudden illness or a callback for a TV show, she would have forgiven him.

Instead his eyes widened and he slapped his forehead. "Shit."

Jane stood there, her arms dead hung at her sides like one of Walter's idle marionettes. That he had simply forgotten, absorbed like a kindergartener in his sewing and glue, she couldn't excuse.

"It was of you," she said.

The Puppeteer's Daughters

"What?"

"My drawing." Jane spoke around the constriction in her throat. "It's of you."

She had wanted to surprise him.

Walter's shoulders sank. "Listen kiddo, I'm really sorry. I'll make it up to you."

"You can't," she stated plainly. That moment, so looked forward to, was gone. *If I am ever a parent,* she thought, *I will not forget important events because I am playing.*

She went to her room and cleaned out every item that spoke of creativity. Paint by number kits, bead kits, a potholder loom, her recorder, cloth scraps, needles and thread, journals where she'd tried her hand at teenage poetry. Glue. Her Kodak Instamatic camera, with undeveloped film in it. Her beloved charcoal pencil set. A purge. Her room had never been cleaner. She sat on her shiny chartreuse bedspread and told herself she liked it.

She went to school the next day and changed her elective from art to typing.

Jane squeezed her cell phone so hard it hurt her hand. These so-called artists, self-indulgent, doing what they wanted while responsible people like Jane did all the work. They were selfish: Brett and Pete wasting the money she had spent on Brett's education, Cora playing with puppets while Jane took care of Walter. Walter was the worst of all. The audacity of him requiring her to make a puppet in order to get the inheritance she deserved.

She tossed her phone down. She'd make a puppet, all right. A fucking voodoo doll.

Chapter 15

Cora emerged from the Queens Plaza subway station to a cacophony of industrial sounds: men jackhammering, glass breaking in a dumpster, the beeping of heavy vehicles backing up at a concrete plant. Cement dust clouded the air. She got her bearings and walked north a block, squinting at the address Alice had given her for the custom machine shop. Alice had warned her not to expect a sign.

Cora had brought her servant puppet. She knew basic welding, but her vision for the puppet's mechanism exceeded her abilities. It was like being a child again, with an adult's vision but the motor control of a five-year-old. She remembered clenched fists and red-faced frustration before she built up the skills she needed to carry out the projects she saw in her head. What she hoped was that the machinist could show her what to do so that she could do it herself in the future. She liked building her own pieces. Outsourcing meant a loss of control and ownership.

The street was a hodgepodge of commercial and residential buildings. She found the shop's open bay between an auto repair place and a shabby four-story apartment building. The machinist, Olin Babich, stood at a screaming machine, wearing a welding mask and ear protection. She had to stand in his line of vision and wave to get his attention.

He turned off the machine and removed his gear. He was very tall, at least six-foot-eight, with curly black hair and a day's worth of razor stubble. Cora had called ahead, so he knew to expect her. She showed him the puppet and explained what she was after. "If I could watch you, I think I could do it myself from here out."

"How valuable is your time?" he asked tersely.

She wasn't sure what he meant.

"How valuable is every hour of your time. I make eighty dollars an hour. What do you make?"

She made too much to share.

"Thought so," he said. "Look, I can teach you to work metal, and I will. You'll like doing it. But to get really good at it will take you hundreds of hours you don't have. It takes ten thousand hours to master a craft. Could I come to your studio and put on an Emmy-winning puppet show?"

"No," she said. For one thing his hands were enormous. They would rip the seams of most of the puppets at Gray Steed.

"Right," he said, "and I wouldn't try." He examined the puppet she had brought. "I think I get what you want. Platinum or titanium costs more but they're lighter, easier for you to hold overhead for long periods."

She bristled. "I'm stronger than you think."

"Metals are like wood. Different metals have different properties. I meant choose the right metal for the job." He tested the puppet's cords. "I might be able to find prefab rings that would work, instead of making them custom. What's your ring size?" He took her hand, his fingers first a gentle pincer at the base of her fingers, then a caliper measuring the breadth of her palm. Cora felt a lurch in her stomach like an elevator landing.

"I don't know my ring size," she said, sounding stupid to herself. "Rings get in the way."

She let him turn her hand over. "Look at all your calluses," he said.

Warmth from his touch seemed to flow down Cora's forearm. She jerked her hand away to stop the spread and snapped, "I'm a puppeteer, not a hand model."

"It's cool," he said. "They're working hands. Like mine." He spread both hands to show her his own rough surfaces. "Leave the machining and metallurgy to me. Should only take a couple of weeks."

Cora thought of all the fairy tales that featured encounters with copper, silver, and gold, each metal more alluring than the last. "Okay," she said, and they shook on it, Olin's giant hand enveloping her small one, both of them holding on slightly longer than necessary.

On the train ride back, she whispered *metallurgy* under her breath, a word she may never have uttered aloud in her life. It sounded magical, like *alchemy*, the syllables dripping like water off a rock. And *titanium*. The name evoked a Shakespearean faerie queen.

She needed to get a grip on herself.

Before returning to the office, Cora went by Neiman Marcus, a store she frequented, and where her face and purchasing power were known. There, a yellow silk scarf slid into her overcoat pocket, her sleight of hand so deft the security cameras didn't capture it. The dexterity required for puppeteering translated well to shoplifting. It was a lovely scarf. She would give it to Alice for her upcoming birthday.

Chapter 16

In the kindergarten pickup line, Madison's teacher, Miss Anne, helped Madison into Rosie's car and fastened her seat belt. "Don't forget to tell your mommy about the dance recital."

Madison handed Rosie a note. The little dance class she took during school hours was putting on a show. "I need a cowgirl hat and a hobby horse," Madison said.

"Walmart has them cheap." Miss Anne closed Madison's door and waved goodbye.

Rosie pulled away from the curb. She reached back and tickled Madison's foot. "A dance recital, that's exciting. Have y'all been practicing?"

"Yes. I can do my hands like this."

Rosie watched her in the rearview mirror as she rolled one hand over the other, feinting right then left.

"Wow. Cool."

"Our families can all come. Tell Daddy and Aunt Jane and Aunt Cora."

Madison had a storybook view of how close families should be. Rosie doubted Jane would want to come to Madison's dance performance and Cora wasn't going to fly down for it. But on impulse Rosie decided to call her mother.

She put her phone on speaker and let Madison punch in the number, for practice. It was important for kids to know how to use a phone.

"Dispatch," Kiki's cigarette voice said. The Lacy Street Rehabilitation Center where Kiki lived ran a moving company to help support itself. Kiki was the lead dispatcher.

"Hi Mama," Rosie said. The word "Mama" always sounded strange when applied to Kiki but Rosie doggedly used it.

"Rosie?"

"Yeah, it's me. I just picked Madison up from kindergarten and they're having a little dance recital in a couple of weeks. Refreshments and such. I wondered if you'd like to come?"

"Honey, you know I don't leave this place. Too much temptation out there in the real world."

"But Madison's growing up so fast. It'd be cool if you could see her dance. I could come get you and then take you right back after, no stops."

"You don't get it, honey. I was—"

"I know, you were living in a box."

"Good. So you do understand." Another call came in on Kiki's headset. "I gotta go. Send me pictures, okay?" Kiki hung up.

"She never comes," Madison said.

"But we'll keep asking." It was good that Madison had never known the disruptive Kiki, but Rosie still felt the hole of Kiki's absence. She would have liked to have a mother.

The puppets weren't the only magical objects on Ginkgo Street. Jane's mother, Ernestine, an enormous, mumu-wearing woman whose ears peeked out through stringy hair, had made Jane a multi-storied doll apartment building out of wooden apple crates. Each room was wallpapered from a sample book, with tiny furnishings. It filled one wall of the hall at Ginkgo Street.

The Puppeteer's Daughters

Rosie was playing with the dollhouse the day Kiki came. Jane had sequestered herself in her room and Ernestine was in the backyard garden picking tomatoes. Rosie heard footsteps mounting the wooden stairs and Kiki walked in the front door without knocking. She came over to where Rosie knelt on the floor. "Hey, baby." Her smile showed rotting front teeth.

Rosie hadn't seen Kiki in months, ever since Rosie's mamaw got the restraining order. She felt the tight feeling that always clutched her tummy when Kiki was around. It came from not knowing what Kiki would do next.

Kiki's eyes darted around the room. She had scratched long red marks into her arms. "Look at the pretty dollhouse." She began rooting through the rooms, messing them up.

There was nothing valuable in the dollhouse. Ernestine had created it with love over the years from the opposite of valuable. Remnants of puppet fur served as wall-to-wall carpet. She had shaped tiny dishes from Sculpey clay. There were a few pieces of plastic doll furniture from Ernestine's childhood: a piano, a dining room table and chairs, two hard blue beds, but the rest Ernestine had made with her clever hands, of Popsicle sticks and cardboard.

Kiki had stolen Rosie's toys before. At Christmas she had shown up with a man, and when they left, Rosie's Happy Holidays Barbie was missing with its box. Rosie's grandmother had cried about that because she couldn't afford to replace it. It had puzzled Rosie why the man and Kiki would want her doll, until Mamaw explained they would return it to Walmart for cash. That's when Mamaw went to court for the restraining order and taught Rosie how to dial 911.

Kiki held up the piano to examine it then tossed it down. She flung furnishings out of the dollhouse and onto the floor. "Look at this shit."

"Stop it!" Rosie yelled. Jane would be mad.

Jane came out of her room at the end of the hall. "What's going on?"

"Where's Walter?" Kiki asked.

"At the TV station," Jane said.

Ernestine came in the back door, breathing hard. She set her gardening basket on the counter and whipped her Tino puppet off her hand. "You shouldn't be here, Kiki."

"Walter owes me money. For child support."

"I write those checks to Rosie's grandmother."

"She's *my* kid." Kiki bent low in front of Rosie, as if summoning a dog. "You want to come with me, Rosie, honey?" Her breath was foul. Before she could touch Rosie, Jane grabbed Rosie's hand and pulled her into the kitchen behind Ernestine.

Kiki turned and knocked down the apple crates. She stomped on one until it splintered, her hair flying.

Ernestine picked up a rolling pin and slapped it in her palm. "Get out of my house before I knock the living shit out of you."

"You fat bitch," Kiki said.

"I may be fat but I'm fast." Ernestine started toward Kiki like a mama sow.

As impaired as she was, Kiki was smart enough to run. She slammed out the door. Ernestine chased her halfway down the wooden steps. Jane and Rosie watched from the top.

The Puppeteer's Daughters

Kiki got in her car, which rode low in the back, her worldly possessions blocking the rear window. She dinged the mailbox as she pulled away and veered out into the street.

Rosie sank to the steps and wailed. She had brought a monster into the Ginkgo Street house. Ernestine and Jane would never want Rosie back again.

Ernestine headed for the phone in the kitchen. "Walter needs to do something about that bitch."

Jane sat down cross-legged next to Rosie at the top of the steps. "Come here." She pulled Rosie into her lap. "It's okay."

"The dollhouse." Rosie's words came in great gulpy hiccups. "You'll be mad at me."

"Shh," Jane said. "Shh, I'm not mad."

ROSIE POKED A STRAW IN A JUICE BOX AND PASSED IT TO MADison in the back seat.

In the fundraising video on the Lacy Street Rehabilitation Center's website, Kiki, sober, told her story, starting with, "I was livin' in a box." Rosie watched it sometimes online. It was professionally produced, with flattering lighting. Kiki wouldn't leave the Lacy Street campus, even on a weekend pass. She didn't come when Madison was born. Rosie had to go to her. Kiki had smiled at Madison but hadn't tried to hold her, as if she were a stranger in line at the grocery store instead of the baby's grandmother.

It was like somebody had locked Kiki in a tower, only she'd come to call the tower home.

Chapter 17

I n fairy tales, the youngest daughter is always the good one.
Jane was not the youngest daughter.

The manila envelope arrived on Thursday afternoon. As she dug it and an AARP solicitation out of her mailbox, the young man who lived in the condo below her called out, "Hey, neighbor!" with a friendly wave before he unlocked his door. Most of the people who lived in the complex were young singles. Jane hadn't realized that when she bought the place. The one time she'd gone down to the workout room in her sweats with thoughts of working on her arm flab, the preening among the youngsters had run her right out of there. She didn't know her neighbors' names, and she didn't care to. She did like her second-floor condo, which came furnished with a white leather couch that she could never have owned when she lived with Pete and the boys. And she liked that someone else mowed the grass and fixed anything that broke.

She took her mail inside, recycled the AARP card, and looked at the envelope. It was from the lab that had done the paternity test.

Jane hadn't expected so quick a response. The envelope had heft, more than one page enclosed. Whatever it held could change her life. And probably not for the better. In Jane's experience, change rarely improved things. Her divorce and Brett's dropping out of school were cases in point.

If the new daughter were a child, it meant more responsibility for Jane, more paperwork, one more person for whom she had to manage things. Jane sometimes, with guilt, imagined the freedom she could expect when Walter passed on. But she knew her luck, or lack thereof. The mother of Walter's love child wouldn't be a CPA. She would be a Luciana or a Kiki. Self-absorbed or useless. It would be Jane who would have to look out for the new half-sister's interests, make sure she got a good education, invite her, however reluctantly, to holiday gatherings. If she had to worry about a child, she would never be free.

And a new sister meant less for Jane. Less money, a smaller claim on her father.

Ernestine and Walter's divorce decree allowed Ernestine to stay in the Ginkgo Street house until Jane graduated high school, then the house would be sold. Walter bought an apartment in Manhattan near his new creative company, and for two years didn't bother removing any of his belongings from Ginkgo Street. His marionettes still hung in the basement, his puppet-making supplies mingled with Ernestine's in the sewing room. He even left his clothes. It was as if he had shed his old skin. They would see him on TV sometimes, or in newspaper photos when he was spotted at clubs in New York. He dressed in cool-looking Armani suits, and his hair, which Ernestine used to cut with a Norelco home barber kit, was now professionally trimmed, as were the wild eyebrows Jane had once drawn. Walter had become hip. Expensive-looking women began to appear on his arm. One in particular, Venezuelan model Luciana Escobar, had affixed herself to Walter's left elbow by Jane's junior year of high school.

The Puppeteer's Daughters

Jane came home one day to find Ernestine going through magazines and tabloids from the grocery store rack, scrubbing through Walter and Luciana's faces with a black marker.

"That bitch better stop spending my money."

Jane should have been sympathetic, maybe even tried to get her mother some help, but as a teenager all she felt was contempt.

Walter married Luciana when she got pregnant with Cora. He invited Jane and her friend Avril to come to New York City that summer for the grand opening of Gray Steed's new studio space and to meet the baby. Jane would spend a week with Avril's family at the Jersey Shore beforehand, then she and Avril would take a bus into Manhattan for the celebration. Jane didn't think much about meeting the new baby. Her mind was on getting a tan at the beach and her first visit to New York.

On the big day, Jane and Avril arrived at Gray Steed's space on East 68th Street, where adults milled around on the sidewalk. Some were dressed as if Studio 54 was their next stop, but she spotted Alf, as schleppy as ever in a patched tweed coat and jeans.

"Janey!" Alf gave her a big hug. He led Jane and Avril inside, introducing Jane as Walter's daughter to the people they passed. They took an elevator to the top floor. The doors opened on a spacious studio with high, exposed ceilings and a polished hardwood floor. Side rooms off the main space held audiovisual equipment and the bright bodies of puppets.

Walter and Luciana, with the baby, stood talking to guests near a temporary partition at the back of the room.

Avril grabbed Jane's arm so hard it hurt and pointed to men selecting beer from an ice bucket in the corner. "Look! That's Jim Henson!"

"Yeah, and Frank Oz and Caroll Spinney—he does Big Bird." Jane had met them at Puppeteers of America conferences when she was little. She remembered Walter and Ernestine doing improv with Muppeteers and every other type of puppeteer imaginable, professionals and amateurs performing marionettes, walkarounds, rod puppets, Bunraku, animatronics. Jane herself, up past her bedtime, dancing barefoot on the periphery with a puppet she'd made from a tongue depressor.

"Oh my God!" Avril said.

Jane shrugged, playing it cool. "No big deal."

"Your dad hasn't stopped talking about you coming up for this," Alf said. Jane wondered if it were true. A waiter handed her and Avril punch from a tray. They followed Alf over to Walter.

"It's my eldest!" Walter said.

Luciana smiled at Avril. "You must be Jane. I've heard so much about you."

"*I'm* Jane," said Jane. Hadn't Walter even showed Luciana a picture of her?

"Darling, forgive me. I'm so sleep-deprived with Cora I'm not thinking straight." Luciana kissed the air beside Jane's cheeks. She didn't look sleep-deprived. She looked gorgeous.

Jane let Walter give her a one-armed hug. "Meet your little sister."

Jane peered at the baby. Cora looked like every other baby, only better dressed, with little green leather shoes that probably cost more than the size nines Jane was wearing. "She's cute," Jane said. Cora squealed.

"See? She likes you already," Walter said.

The room filled with guests, some puppeteers Jane recognized, others people Luciana knew from the fashion industry.

Walter clapped his hands. "Let's get this party started. Alf, you wanna help me move the partition?" He and Alf pushed the retractable partition to the wall. Jane gazed with delight at what it revealed: an exact replica of the marionette stage from Jane's basement.

The detail was amazing. The frog prince and ugly duckling looked exactly the same, only less dusty. There was the soldier with its tinderbox. Walter reached for the twin of his gypsy princess puppet and made her walk along the floor and cock a hip toward the crowd. Her feet clicked on the polished hardwood.

"It's just like the real one," Jane said.

Avril moved closer to the stage. "Jane, it *is* the real one. See the teeth marks on the soldier's shoe?" Avril's little brother had gnawed the shoe one day when Avril and Jane were supposed to be watching him.

"They must have copied the teeth marks too," Jane said, but a bad feeling rose in her chest. She examined the stage. She knew the stories behind its scuffs and chipped paint. Her fingerprints were on the controls that hung like a field of military crosses above the rail. If the stage was here, it was no longer at her house. She had a sudden sensation of sitting in a tree while someone hollowed out its base with a backhoe. The tree would crack and fall at the next wind and she would go with it.

"What do you think?" Walter asked her. "Looks pretty good here, huh?"

He must have come for it, or sent someone for it, while Jane was with Avril at the Jersey Shore. Jane hadn't spoken to Ernestine since they left Raleigh. She imagined her mother standing by as Walter finally retrieved his things, emptying the house of every scrap and button that had been his. Ernestine hadn't worn her Tino puppet since Walter moved out, but in Jane's mind her mother stood in their patchy yard with the bedraggled yellow puppet on her hand, wind and rain howling around her while men with trucks emptied out the house.

"Are you okay?" Avril said, and Jane found that she was not.

"It's all right," Avril said. "It's not like you played with it anymore."

Baby Cora laughed out loud, the diabolical sound echoing off the studio's high ceiling.

"There's our little princess," Luciana cooed. She pressed Cora's tiny fingers to her lips and kissed them.

"Those look like puppeteer hands to me," Alf said.

Jane's fruit punch couldn't mask the foul taste of jealousy that burned the back of her throat.

Rosie's birth hadn't robbed Jane of anything. There had been little to take and Jane headed the queue. Now their father had something to give, and Cora had her little baby hands out, prepared to snatch it all.

⁂

IN HER KITCHEN, JANE CLUTCHED THE LAB'S UNOPENED ENVE-lope. She started to loosen its flap, then stopped.

The Puppeteer's Daughters

If she opened the envelope she would have to tell Cora and Rosie. If she left it sealed, no such obligation would trigger. She propped the envelope behind bills that awaited her attention on the kitchen counter.

It wasn't that she wouldn't share it with her sisters. She simply wouldn't share it yet.

Chapter 18

The raindrops that beaded on Cora's office window couldn't prevent sunlight from slipping past clouds and skirting across facades and rooftops. Cora stopped working, closing out Gray Steed's budget spreadsheets. This was the sort of day when Sabine would return to the park. Sabine didn't come when the rain was hard or cold, but a spring shower like this might bring her out.

By the time Cora got downstairs the rain had vanished. In Central Park, she sidestepped puddles along the path and found Sabine in her usual spot near the *Alice in Wonderland* sculptures. Sabine had laid a plastic garbage bag on a wet bench so she could sit. Her wheeled cart offered cheap black umbrellas for ten bucks.

Sabine was in her eighties, with wispy yellowed hair and watery eyes. Deep wrinkles radiated out from her lips. Her wool coat bore old food stains and always smelled faintly of urine. If it were summer, Sabine might be standing, making her marionette, Madame Bea, feed peanuts to squirrels to earn tourist dollars. Today Madame Bea rested beside Sabine on the bench, near a dirty Styrofoam cup hand-lettered "Fortune Telling $20."

"I hoped I would see you today." Sabine spoke with a hard-to-place European accent. On different days Cora had heard her tell tourists she was French, German, or Dutch.

"How are you?" Cora worried about Sabine in winter. Sabine wouldn't tell her where she lived or how she got by in the off-season.

"We are well," Sabine said, picking up Madame Bea's control. The marionette rose stiffly as if she had been sitting too long, and hopped down from the bench. Her round head swiveled toward Cora.

When she first met Sabine four years ago, Cora recognized Madame Bea as a Pelham marionette, good quality but abused by a past child owner. She suspected Sabine had rescued the puppet from the trash, where some brat had discarded her when she tangled. Sabine had wrapped Madame Bea's snatched-out hair in a paisley turban and covered her gouged right eye with a jaunty red eye patch.

It was clear no one had trained Sabine. Her manipulation of Madame Bea was clunky, hampered by arthritis, but it worked and Cora respected the gig.

"You're here for your fortune?" Madame Bea croaked.

Cora took a twenty from her wallet and stuffed it in the Styrofoam cup.

"Your palm," requested Madame Bea.

Cora perched on the edge of the wet bench and held out her hand. Madame Bea's wooden arm swung in a circle.

"You are looking for someone. Two someones."

Cora almost closed her palm. Madame Bea's fortunes had always been benign, entertaining. Nothing that tempted Cora to believe. Cora only paid for the readings to help Sabine out.

"The first loved one is trapped, locked away in a place that is dark and still," Madame Bea whispered.

The Puppeteer's Daughters

Cora couldn't help but envision a coffin. For the first time it occurred to her that her missing sister might be dead. The feeling of searching too late sickened her.

"She has been there a long time. I fear for her," Madame Bea said. "I do not think you will find her."

"You're supposed to be upbeat," Cora accused. "Last time you predicted I would eat gelato on my way home."

"And you did," said Madame Bea. "I see what I see."

It started to drizzle again, though the sun still shone.

"Ah, the devil is beating his wife. Always good for business. May I sell you an umbrella?" Sabine asked.

"I own five of your umbrellas," Cora said.

"And yet," Sabine twinkled, holding up a crooked pointer finger, "you don't have a single one with you today. That is the way of umbrellas. They are always where you are not."

Cora peeled off another bill and handed it over. She opened an umbrella above her head with a swoosh.

Sabine patted her leg. "We didn't mean to upset you."

"I'm not superstitious," Cora said, but Madame Bea's words had disturbed her. She shook them off. Of course they would find her sister. She wouldn't share this encounter with Jane and Rosie. Rosie especially would find it ominous.

Cora leaned down and pinched Madame Bea's head string, forcing the puppet to lift her prominent chin and look Cora in the eye. "You said there was a second someone. Who is it?"

Madame Bea's hinged feet dangled above the ground. "A giant," she said.

Chapter 19

In fairy tales, transformations were instantaneous: princes into frogs, magic beans into vines that tickled the clouds, girls into swans. In the real world, transformations took time and hard work, if they happened at all.

Rosie's weight loss was not going well. She did fine at work despite the frosting and butter at the Vonich bakery. But at home, it was hard. When she began the diet, it wasn't too bad. The first few days, weighing out portions and tracking everything had been interesting enough to keep her motivated. Then when that got boring, and she found herself starting to cheat, she added a rubber band on her wrist that she popped when she reached for the refrigerator handle between meals. That had worked for a while but now she found herself ignoring the sting of the rubber band and groping in the fridge for what she wanted, even though the pale underside of her wrist had turned pink. She needed to add another barrier of some kind, one more thing to make her stop and think before she shoved the next bite into her pie hole.

She considered a tattoo, for her finger or the back of her hand. An image that would startle her every time her hand reached for food. A stop sign was too on-the-nose. She needed a symbol that would remind her why she was doing this, what the reward would be if she succeeded. The Chinese symbol for money? Tacky, plus she knew a girl who thought her tramp stamp said "wealth" but found out it really said "rice." Maybe a graduation cap, or a diploma, to symbolize what she hoped for Madison? Or a string of those family decals people put on their back windshields, Rosie and Madison and Jane and Cora and Walter, all one big permanent family.

But tattoos hurt.

For the thousandth time since she'd started the diet, she wondered if it was worth it. But if she could be a full daughter instead of an afterthought, if she could welcome their new sister with the same standing as Jane and Cora, it was worth it.

She called Jane. "Have you heard anything from the lab?" It had been three weeks since Jane requested the records.

Jane took a beat to answer. "They said it could take a while to get his chart out of storage."

Rosie was dying to find their sister. She suspected Jane wasn't as eager.

Rosie decided to visit Walter at the nursing home. Even if he couldn't tell her anything about the fourth daughter, it would get her out of her house and away from the fridge.

When she arrived at Bevins, Walter was seated at a table in the dining room. The staff had given him a magazine. He was slowly ripping a page of it into ribbons, then arranging the torn strips on his placemat.

Rosie kissed him on the cheek. "It's me, Dad. Rosie." She liked to think Walter still recognized her as his people, but she always gave him her name just in case.

She moved the magazine out of his reach to get his attention. "Can you tell me about the other daughter?"

He looked at her expectantly, wanting to please.

"Like, what's her name?"

He scrunched his face up and closed his eyes as if in pain. "Names are hard."

"I know." She tried another tack. "Is she younger than me?"

"Yes," he said, amiable.

She didn't trust his response. "Is she older than me?"

"Yes," he said.

This wasn't working.

He reached out and took Rosie's hand. His fingernails were dirty. She would clean and clip his nails before she left.

"She's a good girl," Walter said. "Like you."

Chapter 20

Enchantresses have an allure that no princess can equal.
When Walter remembered sex with Rosie's mother,
Kiki, he heard calliope music.

At the time he met her, he and his marionettes were
minor celebrities with a spot on a local children's television
show, but Walter wasn't rich yet. He had done a festival one
Saturday at Pullen Park, aware the whole time that the teenage girl who ran the carousel was watching him as she took
tickets.

The park closed at five, parents with strollers streaming
for the exits. Kiki came over while he packed up. Her arms
were tan and hairless, a piece of faded red embroidery thread
tied around her left wrist.

"I seen you on TV," she said. Her wavy hair fell to her
waist. When she bent over to look at his puppets, the smell
of green apple shampoo and a glimpse of dark areola beyond
the V-neck of her shirt gave Walter an erection. She noticed
and laughed, a sound like silver bells. "Come on, then." She
beckoned toward the carousel's control room.

Walter had never cheated on Ernestine. Ernestine was his
first, willing to fuck him when he was a skinny nerd with no
experience. He followed Kiki. Her white shorts barely covered her perfect round ass. In the control room, she unzipped
his jeans and ripped them down, pushed him into the opera-
tor's chair and straddled him, laughing wildly. He could feel

her pelvic bones—a novelty, since Ernestine's bones had long ago disappeared into padding. Kiki reached behind him and pushed the control switch. Horses circled them faster and faster, chestnut and bay visible through the control room's green metal grate. Calliope music swelled as he came, in the absolute best, most resounding orgasm of his life.

And of course, she got pregnant.

She told him by phone, nonchalant, because her mother made her. She kept the baby, because her mother made her.

Ernestine was livid, but they couldn't afford to separate. He moved into the sewing room.

Jane was seven when Rosie was conceived. Ashamed, he had to explain to her that he had fathered a child with another woman.

"Will it be a boy or a girl?" Jane asked.

"I don't know."

"I hope it's a girl. Boys are stupid," Jane said.

Walter didn't disagree, but he couldn't stop thinking about sex with Kiki. He went to find her one evening as the park closed. The new swell of her breasts and belly made him desire her even more than before, but Kiki said no. "It'll never be as good as that one time," she said. "You'd just be chasin' the tiger."

Kiki was done with him, but his fling with her had taught him something. There were women out there—attractive, young women—willing to have sex with him. His days of fidelity to Ernestine were over. He left her when he knew his first big check from the Children's Media Workshop was on its way but before he received it, so he wouldn't have to split it with her in the divorce settlement.

The Puppeteer's Daughters

Walter kept his memory of the girl Kiki separate from who Kiki became later, first a manipulative, ravaged drug addict, then the docile middle-aged woman she was when sober. They were so different; the Kiki who had fucked him in the control room might as well be dead. For years after their encounter, Walter would go to Pullen Park in the off-season and stand by the carousel, trash blowing around his feet. He could swear he heard calliope music, even when the horses remained winter-still.

Chapter 21

Jane's childhood friend Avril called. "You aren't going to believe this. Your dad is here."

"Here where?" Jane asked her.

"On Ginkgo Street. I looked out my window and he was standing by the mailbox at your old house. I thought I'd time traveled."

"My dad is at Bevins," Jane said.

"Honey, I'm standing with him right now. I figured you'd want to get over here."

"Is he okay?"

"He's upset. He says he's looking for his daughter, so I told him I'd call you."

"How did he get there?"

"The neighbor who owns your house said she saw somebody drop him off. She's as baffled as I am."

"I'll be right there." Jane's heart pulsed. She got in her car and called the director of nursing at Bevins as she drove. "*Where* is my father?"

"We were just about to notify you," the director said. "We're searching the campus. He isn't strong enough to get far."

"Wanna bet?" Jane said.

The director paused. "How did you know he was missing?"

"Not from you!" Jane said. "A friend of mine found him. She's with him at our old house, three miles from your facility. How the hell did you let that happen?"

"Rosie visited him this afternoon. We thought at first she'd taken him outside for some air."

"I'm going to get him. When I bring him back, I want a meeting with you and the CEO and whoever the hell else needs to be there to give me a full explanation."

When she reached Ginkgo Street, Avril was standing with Walter and another woman in the driveway of Jane's old house. Jane hardly recognized the house now that the current owner had painted over the orange and purple with a respectable tan. She parked and got out. Avril spoke soothingly to Walter. "See, Mr. Gray? I told you she was on her way."

Walter barely glanced at Jane. He was agitated. "She's here. She has to be here."

"It's me, Dad," Jane said. He must mean her. Jane was his Ginkgo Street daughter. Was she so changed that he couldn't connect her to the girl she had been?

"But there's another one." He was crying now. Jane's eyes teared up.

"The house is the wrong color," Walter sobbed. He had soiled himself. His adult diaper couldn't contain the smell. The homeowner took a step back, wrinkling her nose. Grief for her father squeezed Jane's throat.

Jane called Rosie.

"He seemed fine this afternoon. I asked him about the other daughter but he couldn't tell me anything," Rosie said.

"You asked him about the daughter? For God's sake Rosie, that's what put it in his head. What were you thinking?"

"I didn't expect a simple question to make him run away!"

"Don't talk to him about it again," Jane said.

"You don't want to find her," Rosie accused. "You wish you'd never heard of her. But she's out there, and if you don't want to lead the search, get out of the way and me and Cora will."

In the driveway, Walter wept, snot covering his face. Avril tried to comfort him.

"I'm standing here with our father, who has shit his pants, and I have to get him back to Bevins. I do not have time for any additional shit from you right now." Jane hung up.

Avril helped her lead Walter to her car. Jane fastened his seatbelt with shaking hands, listening to him whimper, "Where is she? Where is she?"

⁊

AFTER SHE GOT WALTER BACK TO BEVINS AND CLEANED UP, with a month's room charge knocked off his bill in exchange for not suing, Jane called Avril to let her know he was okay. "They think he must have talked a nursing home visitor into believing he was a visitor too, and somehow remembered the Ginkgo Street address to ask for a ride. He'll have a bracelet now that will set off an alarm if he tries to leave. Thank God you saw him. He could still be wandering the neighborhood."

"What's this about the daughter?" Avril asked.

Jane explained.

"Maybe he means me?" Avril said. "I was at your house enough growing up."

"I don't think so," Jane said. "He's missing someone." And it wasn't Jane.

Chapter 22

Cora listened to Rosie sniffle on the phone. "Jane thinks it's my fault."

"Nonsense. Who could have guessed he was capable of escaping?" Jane always had to assign blame.

"Should we not look for her?" Rosie asked. "If it's just going to cause trouble?"

Cora remembered Madame Bea's fortune and shuddered slightly. "No, we don't give up, though there's not much we can do until we see the lab records." Cora tried to distract Rosie. "Hey, you know how Dad wanted his puppets to go to the Smithsonian? I spoke to a curator there and they want to do an exhibit now. It would be a two-year loan, of the Czech marionettes and Dad's early pieces. I have a photo of the Ginkgo Street basement they'll replicate. Is it okay to loan your swan puppet?"

"I don't know. That puppet might be all I get when he dies," Rosie said.

"They'll take good care of it."

"Well, all right."

"Don't let Jane get to you," Cora said, wanting to offer comfort.

"I'll try not," Rosie said.

After Rosie's call, Cora went to find Alf, whose office was two floors below hers at Gray Steed's headquarters. She walked through a studio where puppeteers in leotards rehearsed the choreography for a new musical number, their puppetless arms moving like synchronized cobras above their heads. She could feel the puppeteers tense as she walked by, like troops when a general inspects. It made Cora tired, being in charge.

She thought of the day nearly four years ago when her father had called her and Alice and Alf in to tell them about his diagnosis. "My gray matter is toast. I know you've noticed. I need to hand things over before anyone else sees it."

Alice stifled a sob and reached out to Walter. He squeezed her hand. Alf wiped his forehead.

"I'm leaving Cora in charge," Walter said.

"What? No!" Cora couldn't run his company. There was too much she didn't yet know.

"Alice will help you. So will Alf, right?"

Alice nodded.

"Fuck, man," Alf murmured. "Fuck, I'm so sorry."

"You can do this, Cora." Walter cleared his throat. "Don't let Gray Steed disappear. Go on now, Alf and I have to wrap up some loose ends on the *Zeno and Friends* special."

Cora stepped out into the hall with Alice. "What am I going to do?"

Tears streamed down Alice's cheeks. She didn't try to stop them. "We'll do as he says."

❧

DOWNSTAIRS, ALF WAS IN HIS OFFICE. FRAMED PHOTOS HUNG on the wall behind him, of Alf and Walter on the set of the Uncle Lee children's hour; the two of them accepting an Emmy for *Zeno and Friends*; and one Alf had taken at Jane's wedding of Walter with Cora, Jane, and Rosie. To Jane's annoyance, Walter had insisted his gypsy princess marionette be in the shot, wearing a puff-sleeve gown of the same peach chiffon as Rosie's and Cora's bridesmaid and flower girl dresses.

Alf was absorbed in his laptop. He was wearing a plaid sports jacket and some oily hair product. Cora was fond of Alf, but she'd always thought he gave off more of a used-car-salesman vibe than a puppeteer vibe.

She knocked on the doorframe.

"Co Co!" He used his annoying childhood nickname for her. He shut his laptop and came around to give her a hug. "Good to see you! What are you doing down here in the trenches?"

"I have something to ask you," she said.

"Yeah?" His eyes flitted to his computer.

She told him about Walter's reference to a fourth daughter at the birthday party. "Did he ever say anything to you?"

Alf shook his head. "Sometimes he'd tell me things I wished he hadn't. Other times he'd keep the stupidest things secret." He gave a sad smile. "I miss your dad."

"Me, too," she said. "Don't mention the daughter thing to anyone. If there's nothing to it I don't want to start a rumor."

"Gotcha."

Alf walked her down the hall to the elevator, past rooms where drawers were labeled "noses" and "eyes" and "hair" and writers sat around bouncing jokes off each other. The smell of superglue wafted from the prop room.

Alf pushed the button to summon the elevator. "How's Janey? And Rosie?" He was the only person on earth who could get away with calling Jane "Janey."

"They're good."

"Too bad those girls didn't follow in Walter's footsteps the way you did."

"The world only needs so many puppeteers," Cora said. She waved goodbye as the elevator doors closed.

Rosie might not have gone into puppetry herself, but Cora owed her *Tangled Tales* to Rosie. By the time Cora was six, she had convinced her parents to use Rosie for her babysitter instead of the nanny. Rosie was more malleable than the professionals. Cora could get away with late bedtimes and Cat in the Hat–style mayhem that Rosie patiently picked up after. Rosie would cut Cora's pimento cheese sandwiches into different shapes: squares for Mama Bear, strips for Baby Bear, triangles for that bitch Goldilocks. Cora's mother grumbled about chips and ice cream disappearing during Rosie's shifts, but Cora, as usual, got her way.

The highlight of the night was the puppet show Cora would put on in the playroom with Rosie as the conscripted audience. Cora had the *Blue*, *Red*, and *Yellow Fairy Books* memorized. Rosie sat on the couch while Cora put on the show.

One night, Cora was performing "Diamonds and Toads," particularly proud of the speed with which she could transform the pitiful crone puppet into an angry witch. She had just uttered her favorite line, *"'Well, Mother,' answered the pert hussy, throwing out of her mouth two vipers and two toads,"* when she heard a noise in the audience. She peeped past the puppet stage curtain. Rosie had fallen asleep sitting up and was snoring, her breath a delicate but pronounced *"paaaah."*

Cora could not believe that someone could fall asleep during a performance as riveting as "Diamonds and Toads." The puppet action halted. She cleared her throat. Rosie slept on.

"Welcome back to the *Rosie Show!"* Cora shouted, calculating, correctly, that the utterance of Rosie's name would get her attention. Rosie startled, looking dazed for a moment, unsure where she was until her eyes focused on Cora and the puppets.

"Pay attention, now," Cora chided. Cora had never considered that any audience of hers would be anything but rapt, hanging on her every word. Her parents and nanny had never responded to her shows with less than a standing ovation. Rosie put her fingers to her eyes, literally holding her lids open. Cora was less offended than intrigued. She had been deceived. The world at large might not adore every word or twist of puppet she created. She might have to work to earn an audience's reaction.

Cora started the story over, monitoring Rosie through a slit in the curtain. As the first sister was kind and reaped her reward of bejeweled speech, Rosie stifled a yawn. As the second sister spoke rudely to the rich woman and received the curse of speaking in reptiles and amphibians, Rosie discreetly reached for a *People* magazine, pulling it toward her with one finger to read the cover.

Cora had to do something. At the point where she should

have recited, "and the good sister lived happily ever after," she instead said loudly, "the sister who spoke diamonds married the Prince. The Prince kissed her and choked on one of the diamonds and died."

"Wait, what?" Rosie looked up. Cora had her attention now.

"The other sister married a man named Bob. They opened a bait and tackle shop and lived happily ever after," Cora said.

"That's hilarious," Rosie said.

"Thank you," Cora said.

"How do you even know what a bait and tackle shop is?" Rosie asked.

Cora took the sister puppets off her hands. She had never felt this pleased with herself. "Jane and Pete took me fishing."

"Go figure," Rosie said, chuckling.

That night, after Cora had a bath, Rosie gently combed the tangles out of Cora's hair, still laughing about the bait and tackle bit. Cora wanted to return something to her audience. She met Rosie's eyes in the bathroom mirror and parroted what her mother said about Rosie: "You *do* have a pretty face."

The skin around Rosie's eyes saddened.

Cora's childhood relationship with Rosie had been not so much a sister relationship as a tyrant-serf relationship, Cora realized now. Rosie always half family, half the help. That needed to change.

Cora had stolen the lipstick for Jane and the scarf for Alice. She knew just the thing Rosie would like.

The Puppeteer's Daughters

STEALING THE KNIVES PROVED TO BE A GREATER FEAT THAN slipping some small item into her pocket. Stores locked knives away. One had to ask a salesperson with a key to open the case so that one could examine them closely. The problem was pleasing, like a puzzle, and Cora worked on it with the back of her brain all week. She chose Williams-Sonoma because it was as busy as Christmas all year round. Cora dressed like a tourist and carried full shopping bags into the store. She shadowed a newlywed couple purchasing knives along with several other things with their wedding gift cards. The couple looked like a J. Crew ad, stylish clothing and fresh faces, plenty of money to spend, their heads bent adorably over their list. She followed them to the checkout. The clerk rang up the knife set. Cora set her own bags down on the counter to adjust her load. When she picked them up, with a crook of her pinky, she lifted one more bag than she set down. It was that easy. The couple was still watching the clerk wrap their glassware. Each would assume the other left the store with the knives.

She took the knives to the Gray Steed mailroom. "Anything liquid, fragile, perishable, or potentially hazardous?" asked the young trans man who ran the mailroom.

"No," Cora said. The young man had the same coloring as a young Walter Gray. What if the daughter her father missed had transitioned to male and they should instead be looking for a son?

"Is there something else I can help you with?" the young man asked.

"No," Cora said. "I'm just thinking about the 'what ifs.'"

🐦

ROSIE CALLED CORA WHEN THE KNIVES ARRIVED TWO DAYS LATER. "I love them, but they're so expensive!"

"I used my Verizon points," Cora said, observing that for the first time she had added a lie to her theft. It was interesting how one led to the other. She didn't care for it. She vowed that with future thefts she would not lie. She would be silent, a demure smile if anyone asked how or where she acquired something. And if she got caught, which seemed less and less likely, she would take her punishment.

She indulged for a moment in imagining what it would be like to be taken to the back room by Compliance. She wouldn't deny anything. She would, of course, call her lawyer, but she wouldn't ask him to get her off. She would go to municipal court and sit with all the other criminals until her name was called, and enter a guilty plea. Cora had never been to court, for so much as a traffic ticket. The one citation she'd earned driving too fast to the Hamptons, her father's lawyer had made go away without her having to appear. She was aware that her image of a courtroom came from old episodes of *Law and Order* and that an actual courtroom might be different, somewhat worse and more upsetting. She imagined the smell of a courtroom in winter, wet wool and cigarettes, children crying. People of various ethnic backgrounds and degrees of cleanliness with whom Cora didn't have contact except on the subway—she'd be one of them. It would all be very Dickensian.

But they had to catch her first.

Chapter 23

Rosie sliced an orange with the eight-inch carving knife from the set Cora had sent her, the lovely blade so sharp it hardly made a sound. Her diet plan let her eat as much fruit as she wanted. Oranges were zero points. She had no problem buying healthy food like this at the grocery store. She could do that. Fill her cart with Cutie tangerines that were easy for Madison to peel, and the Japanese Sumo citrus fruits Vonich carried now, with the leaves left on to prove freshness. She could feel righteous in the checkout line comparing her cart's contents to the customers ahead and behind. No processed meats for her, no snack crackers, no alcohol. Everything from the outside perimeter of the store: fruits and vegetables and skim milk.

But discipline at the moment of purchase did not equate to discipline at the moment of consumption. This perfect orange that Rosie now cupped in her hands, which God had packaged so conveniently and even divided out for her into bite-size portions, did not satisfy. She could eat one or two or three, and they were good. But they left her wanting something more, in a way that a sticky bun from the Vonich bakery did not. Why was that? Why couldn't she convince her brain that an orange was as satisfying as sugar and butter? Rosie had taken home ec instead of chemistry in high school, but she suspected the answer was chemical. Some attribute of fat molecules that made them want to embrace her body and hang on for dear life, while healthier citrus molecules were content to say hi in passing and be on their skinny way.

Rosie ate the orange without enthusiasm, knowing already that when she finished the last section she would reach into the refrigerator for the cake Gary had brought by last night. She sighed. This time of evening was the worst, after Madison went to bed. A physical force seemed to drag Rosie's body to the kitchen and her hand to her mouth. It occurred to her that this was how it must've felt for Kiki, when the stakes were losing Rosie if she kept using. It was so hard to give up immediate gratification for the bigger future prize. It made Rosie feel more sympathy for Kiki.

Kiki was livin' in a refrigerator box. Rosie was livin' in the refrigerator.

She decided to go for a walk, to get away from her fridge and cabinets. She texted her neighbor to let her know. Leaving Madison alone wasn't the best parenting, but she bet she wasn't the first single mom to do it.

She set out down the lone country road her house was on, past the cemetery and into town. Rosie wasn't afraid or nervous—her mother's family had lived on this stretch for generations. She knew the shadows at all times of day or night. She didn't have appropriate shoes and her feet hurt—a lot—but at least she wasn't snacking. And if she walked every night, a time might come when her thighs didn't rub together and she could make the uphill slope by the cemetery without stopping for breath. The night was balmy for early spring. Droplets hung in the air and settled on her hair and skin.

She drew near town. Everything in Deaverville closed at five p.m., which was good. Otherwise she'd be tempted to buy a snack somewhere. Under the streetlight in front of the Exxon, a figure sat on the curb, head in hands. Rosie walked closer and the person looked up. It was no one Rosie knew. They wore overalls and a flannel shirt. Their head was too small for their body. Their short hair was mashed flat in the back as if it had been slept on. It was an older person but Rosie couldn't tell if it was a man or a woman. She also couldn't tell whether they were taking the night air or might need help.

Rosie took the opportunity to stop and catch her breath. "Hey there," she said. "You doing okay tonight?"

"I reckon so." The voice was female.

"Do you live nearby?" Rosie hated to be nosy but this woman might have wandered off like Walter, and gotten lost.

The woman waved a thin hand without pointing in any particular direction. "Not too far."

"Can I help you up?"

The woman reached out her arms like a child. Rosie pulled her to her feet and steadied her before letting go.

"I know you," the woman said.

Rosie was sure she did not. "I'm Rosie Calhoun. What's your name?" She might know the woman's people.

"One wish," she thought she heard the woman say.

"What?"

"Vonich. Cake. You made a cake for my grandson."

"Oh," Rosie said, strangely disappointed. For a brief moment she had felt the warmth of the words *I know you*. Oh, to be known by someone. But this was just a Vonich customer.

Loud footsteps sounded in the moist air and a man came trotting up Main Street, in pajama pants, an undershirt, and shoes with the laces untied. "Granny," he called out. He reached them, panting. "Granny." He turned to Rosie. "She's not supposed to be out here by herself. I turned around and she was gone."

"I sat down to rest a spell and couldn't get back up is all," the woman said.

Rosie introduced herself to the grandson.

"Thanks for helping her," he said.

"No problem. I have an older person of my own who wanders," Rosie told him.

The man took his granny's arm and guided her across the street and down the sidewalk. The old lady looked back over her shoulder at Rosie and held up one finger. The last two streetlights on that side were burnt out, giving the illusion that the two figures disappeared as they passed the furniture store.

Chapter 24

When Cora returned to the machine shop the second time, Olin wasn't working in the bay. The door to a back room was open. She stuck her head in. The room held ceiling-high sculptures made of metal objects soldered together. If she looked close, she could identify bicycle rims, tin cans, chains, but if she took in the sculptures as a whole they gave the impression of people or, in one case, a giant bird. Some surfaces were polished, others rusty, the patina as calculated as the object placement.

Olin stood polishing a small piece of metal with a cloth.

"These are incredible," Cora said.

He looked up. "Hey."

She walked closer, laying a hand on the nearest sculpture. "I know a folk art gallery in Chelsea that would kill for these."

"I'm not a folk artist," he said, still polishing. "I'm schooled. BA from Parsons, one year of an MFA in sculpture before I realized I didn't need a master's, since I was never going to teach. I make more money from my shop than I would teaching art. And when I flip my door sign to 'Closed' at night I don't think about work at all."

She envied that.

"You didn't think a mere machinist could be an artist," he goaded.

"I didn't think anything." *Why would I?* she thought. *Why would I think of you at all?*

"You have your art on the side, I have mine." He set the piece of metal down. "I'll go get your job. I think you'll be pleased."

When he left, she looked at the metal he had been polishing. It was a star, one of three, each about two inches in diameter, with a pleasing lack of symmetry. She stroked one. Its surface sent a chill up her spine. Cora wanted it. This bright bauble was not for her sisters or Alice. She, the magpie, would keep it for herself.

In fairy tales, one can steal from a giant and flee.

She slipped the top star into her pocket, felt its satisfying weight. She took the second star and listened to it clink when it hit the first.

Cora reached for the third star. A hand encircled her forearm, blocking her reach. Olin's stern eyes stared down at her. "Mustn't take what isn't yours."

In the dim air between her face and his, microscopic metal shavings flashed, swirling with dust motes in a shrapnel dance.

Cora placed her finger in the bowl of his clavicle. His pulse beat with hers in the pad of her fingertip.

With a long exhale he loosened her ponytail. Her hair dripped through his fingers like sand.

❧

SHE LAY ON HER BACK BESIDE OLIN IN HIS BED. HIS BEDROOM was clean, austere. Not a room he spent time in. The extra-long mattress functionally comfortable. A heavy quilt that must have been homemade, with a smell musty but sweet, like straw. A few books on modern sculpture, and his keys,

122

just two, on the nightstand next to the puppet mechanism he had made for her. Cora felt calm, relaxed, as if she had had the best sleep of her life, though she and Olin hadn't slept. Olin's eyes were closed, his breathing slow, but he was awake, his broad palm resting on her stomach.

His apartment was in the building next to his shop. Sounds from the street permeated the window: a truck idling, men shouting. She measured herself relative to Olin. Stretched to her full length her body met his from where her head rested in the crook of his shoulder to his mid-shin. The difference in size hadn't mattered.

Olin rested his chin on the top of her head. "Do you have to go? Anybody waiting for you? A husband? A cat?"

"Only my vice president."

"So stay."

His quilt's otherworldly weight seemed to hold her in place. "What would we do if I stayed?"

"Get food at the Dominican place across the street. Test out your puppet. Then you go."

"I have a meeting."

He reached out a long arm for the metal skeleton that would move her puppet. He held it while she slipped the rings over her fingers.

At first, the mechanism's operation was almost too smooth, like ice-skating with sharp blades after learning on dull ones. She had to slow her movements down or else the speed, the lack of friction, would derail her. She found her ears straining for the click of rings and jangle of cords but there were no such sounds to hear. The puppet's movements were as silent as air.

"How did you do this? It's perfect," she said.

"Are you sure? Because I can adjust it. You could leave it here another day. Come back for it tomorrow."

"It's perfect." She got out of bed and dressed, leaning over him for a last kiss that tasted like a blend of precious metals.

He stretched his arms over his head. Cora could count his ribs. "Come back anyway," he said. "Bring me another puppet."

When Cora arrived at Gray Steed, Alice was in Cora's office. "The budget numbers for *Birdlandia* look feasible. Do we want to pitch it to Disney?"

"Yes," Cora said. "But keep it quiet." She slipped the metal skeleton inside her servant puppet's cloth body and brought it to life. "Look what I have."

"New man?" Alice asked.

"What?" Cora said.

"Your hair," Alice said. Cora touched her head and realized her hair was still free of its ponytail.

Chapter 25

Jane went by to see her mother. Ernestine spent most of her time in her apartment. The apartment wasn't big enough for all her junk. Piles of clothes and craft projects filled corners and spilled from doorways. Jane had spoken to her mother about the tripping hazard, but Ernestine had ignored her.

Jane tussled with Ernestine yearly to cull her stuff. *No, you do not need copies of your phone bills dating back to Alexander Graham Bell. Or income tax returns from when the Sixteenth Amendment was passed.* Last fall when she'd shown up at Ernestine's for the annual enforced clearing out, she and Ernestine had wrestled over a plastic milk jug of old maps her mother had saved. "You don't travel these days. And even if you did, these maps are so old they aren't accurate—they'd get you lost."

"I *like* them," Ernestine said.

"They lead to places that don't exist anymore," Jane said.

"Exactly!" Ernestine jerked the maps from Jane's grasp and clutched them to her chest. "I can make collages with them."

Jane wished Ernestine had other children. Cora and Rosie were of limited use as siblings because they weren't on the hook to share Ernestine's care.

Today when Jane arrived, her mother had pulled everything out of the living room closet. She was sitting at the table digging in a box.

"What are you doing?" Jane asked.

"Looking through the home movies your father left behind. Cora asked if I had any the Smithsonian might want."

"Cora called you?"

"Here." Ernestine pushed the box toward Jane. Movie reels from the seventies, and VHS tapes from the eighties, some labeled, most not. "He recorded his puppet shows to perfect them."

Walter spent money they didn't have on top-of-the-line movie cameras with audio, not to capture their family moments, but to evaluate his performances, first in real time on a monitor, then afterward on video like a coach post-game.

"Have Pete convert these to see if there's anything on there the Smithsonian might pay me for," Ernestine said.

"Do you need money, Ma? I can give you money."

"I don't want your money. I want his."

Jane took the box. After Pete lost his job as a video editor for the public relations agency and he and Jane divorced, Pete had parlayed his obsession with old recording devices into a business, converting people's wedding videos to digital. His Videomeister store was open four days a week, leaving him time for his other interests—music and pot.

"Can you take them today?" Ernestine asked.

"Sure," Jane said.

"Give Pete my love," Ernestine said. Jane saw her mother as if for the first time. She had grown smaller, her hair thinner. Jane saw that she was lonely.

She remembered Ernestine in a yellow-flowered tent dress with Tino on her arm, teaching children at a festival to make puppets from found objects. Spoons, leaves, brown paper lunch bags. Scarves and tennis balls. Egg-carton cat-erpillars. When her parents divorced, most of the puppeteers who had formed their community apologetically followed Walter. He was the rising star in New York, where puppe-teers could earn a living. The few who sided with Ernestine were elderly now, not able to visit; some had passed away.

"Do you want to catch a movie this week?" Jane said.

Ernestine shrugged, as if the thought of going out was too much effort. "Nah. But come over again, if you have time."

Jane helped her mother put things back in the closet, then drove downtown to take Walter's movies to Pete. She found parking a few blocks away and carried the box on her hip into Videomeister. She hadn't spoken to Pete since Brett's announcement that he was dropping out of college.

There were no customers in the store. Pete was editing a video, reading glasses down on his nose. The overhead light shone on his bald spot and ratty ponytail. He looked around when she came in and his face lit up, out of old habit, she supposed. "Hey!"

She hefted the box of movies onto the counter. "My mother sends her love and these. Can you convert them and please not charge her, or me?"

Pete looked through the box. "Yes, assuming there's no mold. What are they?"

"Dad's puppets."

"I'll put them on DVDs and a thumb drive, so you can edit the files."

"I'm not going to edit any files. Cora asked my mother

for them. Those two can decide what to do with whatever's on there."

"I'll bring them to you when I'm done," he said.

"I can pick them up."

"It's no problem."

"Suit yourself." She looked around the shop, with its obsolete but vital machinery. Pete bragged that he could convert any electronic file, no matter how old. He even had an ancient computer that could take old floppy disks. Every new means of storing information thought it was the last. How many memories had been lost to obsolescence?

"Have you talked to Brett?" he asked.

"Nope." The silent treatment seemed appropriate when your college senior dropped out just as he was reaching the finish line.

"He likes the band. They're making some money, playing a few festival dates."

"Whatever," Jane said.

"It would mean a lot to him to have your support."

"He's got yours. He doesn't need me."

"Jane." Pete looked at her over his glasses. He always made her the bad guy, he and the boys both. She was done with it.

Pete sighed. "I'll call you when I have these ready."

Jane left the shop. A teenage girl sat on the curb near the intersection, dirty canvas backpack beside her. She wore a do-rag over a self-inflicted crew cut. She had a sunflower tattoo at the base of her neck and piercings in her nose and left eyebrow. Her skin was windburned a red-brown from too much time outside.

"Spare any change?" the girl said, in a tone that was almost bored.

Jane checked her out. The haircut was homemade, but the tattoo and piercings looked expensive. If she could afford body art, why should Jane give her money? The girl didn't even offer a story. Usually the panhandlers on this stretch had a story. Involving the need for a bus ticket to visit a sick mother. Always in Durham, for some reason. Why Durham? Maybe because it was only thirty miles away. It made the request seem small and reasonable, not like a bus ticket to Seattle. Someone ought to do a study on the rhetoric of panhandling.

"Sorry," Jane said, avoiding eye contact. She was stuck with the girl until the light changed.

"I just need enough for a bus ticket," the girl said. "To—"

"Let me guess," Jane interrupted. "Durham."

"How'd you know?" the girl asked.

Jane looked at her directly now. "What do you really want my money for?"

The girl shrugged. "Same stuff you would spend it on. Food. A soda. Tampons would be good."

"Ever thought about working?" Jane said.

"I was busking, but somebody stole my guitar." The girl scratched her head through the do-rag. "One dollar would buy me a bread bun at Jimmy John's."

She was pitiful, younger than Jane's sons. Jane felt herself getting sucked in, but she refused to enable the girl. The light changed. Jane shook her head and started across.

"You'll be sorry!" the girl called after her.

Jane turned around. The nerve of this one.

"Have a blessed day," the girl said.

Jane continued across the street, digging her keys out of her purse as she walked. Just as she was about to step up on the curb, a motorcycle roared by, too close, startling her. She jumped. Her shoe wedged in the gutter grate and her foot twisted. She felt a pop in the top of her foot and then excruciating pain. She lay on the sidewalk, her keys and the contents of her purse scattered, trying to catch her breath around the pain.

She heard a door burst open and running footsteps. Pete knelt beside her. "Jane!"

"My foot," she croaked. He cupped it gently and she screamed.

"You might have broken something," he said. "I'll pull my car around. Sit tight." He sprinted away. A woman passing by helped Jane gather her belongings. Jane looked across the street. The homeless girl was nowhere to be seen.

Chapter 26

Rosie called Cora. "It's her fifth metatarsal."

"That's a toe," Cora said. In the background Rosie could hear horns honking and trucks rumbling by.

"Yeah, but the boot is up to her knee, to stabilize it. She won't be driving for a while. And she can't make it up the steps to her condo."

"Move her into the MacArthur Downs house. Everything she needs is on one level. Jane always wanted to live in the big house. Now's her chance."

"She won't be able to visit Dad. She thinks if family isn't there every day the staff won't treat him right. I should be able to go by most days."

"Maybe I can come down. I'll check my schedule," Cora said.

"That would be awesome." Jane wasn't the easiest person to deal with in the best of times, much less after being stuck inside for days.

After they hung up, Rosie finished pressing a Clemson University pennant to her fridge. Pennants for NC State, Carolina, Wake Forest, and Duke already covered the crack between her side-by-side refrigerator doors. She would have to untape the flags to open her fridge. The idea was to slow herself down enough to make her think about what she ate.

Madison came in from watching *Zeno and Friends* in the

living room. "Mama, why are you taping those flags everywhere?"

"They're college flags. I'm excited about you going to college."

"I'm only in kindergarten."

"It's never too early to start planning." Rosie tested the pennant barricade, tugging on the refrigerator door handle the way she would without thinking when she couldn't sleep at night. The pennants resisted. Rosie was satisfied.

Madison held her arms above her head like a ballerina. "I like the red one best."

"NC State. That's where Grandpa Walter went to college."

"Where'd you go?"

"Me? I didn't go to college."

"Did Daddy?"

"No."

"Then how come you want me to go?"

"Because it's fun. You learn stuff and meet people."

"Why didn't you go?"

"That's a good question," Rosie said. At eighteen, going to college had never crossed her mind. She wasn't crazy about school. She was crazy about Gary, focused on moving in with him the summer after high school graduation. She was already an assistant manager at the Vonich bakery, which seemed like a decent job to her and didn't require a degree. Neither her mamaw nor Walter ever suggested she try college.

"What's it like at college?" Madison said.

Rosie started to answer and then realized she had no idea. "Maybe we'll go visit some so you can see." Did they let five-year-olds on college tours?

"Okay, but not right now. Arlina's coming over to play."

"We've got plenty of time," Rosie said.

As Madison went outside to wait for her friend, Gary called.

"Hey. I got tomorrow afternoon off. How about I come over? We can send Madison next door while we do it."

"I can't tomorrow. I'm taking food to Jane."

"Since when is she more important than me?"

"She broke her foot," Rosie said. "When you break a bone, I'll put you first."

"Well, shit," Gary said.

"You could come over this weekend."

"Can't. Listen, Rosie, Amber's moving into my place this weekend. I'm telling you before you hear it from somebody else."

"She is?" Rosie felt disoriented for a second. Gary had never lived with anybody in the years since they'd split up. "I thought you liked your space," she said.

"I do. It's so she can help me with rent. Work's been slow lately. It doesn't mean anything."

Rosie couldn't think of what to say. She opened her refrigerator door. Scotch tape gave way with a ripping sound. Pennants dangled loose on both sides. She grabbed a can of whipped cream.

"Nothing's going to change between you and me, okay?" Gary promised.

"Okay," she said.

When he hung up, she looked at the can of whipped cream in her hand. The Scotch tape hadn't done its job. She would get something stronger, packing tape or duct tape. She placed the can of whipped cream back on the shelf. It took everything she had.

She'd been with Gary for years before she got pregnant. They had both worked and she couldn't remember ever being short of money. For fun they went out to bars to line dance or stayed at home watching TV. And they had lots of sex.

The house Rosie had inherited from her mamaw seemed big until they had to squeeze in all the baby stuff. The crib wouldn't fit in their bedroom so Rosie set it up in the outer room. She hung wooden cutouts of the Three Little Pigs on the wall behind it, the pigs in blue jackets with bright gold buttons dancing along on their hind legs, no wolf in sight. She shoved the changing table into a corner to make space for a glider rocker.

It wasn't like they were teenagers when they had Madison. They were old enough that Gary should have been able to handle it. Rosie would have been happy to get pregnant sooner but it didn't happen, even though they were haphazard with birth control. Maybe her weight messed with her hormones.

Those first sleep-deprived weeks with Madison were a blur. Gary was good about bringing Madison to Rosie to nurse so all Rosie had to do was roll on her side and pull her T-shirt up. The problem was getting Madison to stop crying at night.

Looking at Madison now, so sweet and eager to please, it was hard for Rosie to believe how hard she'd been to console.

The Puppeteer's Daughters

They'd tried everything. Gary fast-walked her around the living room in her carrier, holding the handle by one hand, the muscles in that arm bulging. Madison would quiet down while he was in motion but start up again when he stopped. They put her in a bouncy chair on the dryer while it ran, to see if the noise and vibration would comfort her. They drove her around in Gary's truck, a trick their friends swore by, but Madison just arched her back and screamed.

They lived in a fog. Gary drove the wrong way down a one-way street he'd traveled on every day of his life. Rosie put Madison in her car seat and went through the drive-throughs at the bank and Taco Bell, not realizing until she got home that she hadn't actually buckled Madison in. It was worse for Gary than Rosie. With maternity leave, she could steal a nap when Madison slept in the afternoon, but Gary had to work. He needed his sleep at night and he wasn't getting it. Rosie could see him crumbling. She tried to shoulder more of the load to help him along, but even if she hopped up as soon as Madison started to cry she couldn't spare him the noise in the small house.

Looking back on it, Rosie wondered if Madison had cried because she was hungry. As big as Rosie's breasts were, she never made a lot of milk. She ran out when Madison nursed and never had extra to pump like some women did. After Gary left and Rosie went back to work, she switched to formula and Madison slept better. It was hard to think that if she'd just fed her baby more those early weeks, Gary might have stayed. Might have.

The night he had enough, their air conditioner window unit broke and the temperature in the house rose to ninety degrees. Gary stripped off his shirt. Sweat dripped down Rosie's chest between her breasts. Madison had been crying for a half hour. They'd fed her and changed her but still she cried.

Rosie remembered that night in black and gray. Faint moonlight slid through the window, erasing the bright colors of the Three Little Pigs above Madison's crib. Gary paced with Madison, growing more and more frustrated. Tension and anger moved across his back, tightened his upper arms, and started to travel down his wrists. Rosie moved to take the baby away from him but somehow where his hands touched Madison he managed to keep them gentle. He laid her in her crib, then dropped to his knees and beat the cushion of the rocking chair with his fists as hard as he could, pounding and pounding. The glider rocked like a wild thing trying to get away.

Rosie felt for Gary but she was terrified too. What if a time came when he wasn't able to stop his rage before it entered his hands? What if he hit Madison, or shook her, or hurled her against the wall?

Gary collapsed with his head buried in his arms on the glider seat. The rocker stilled. Madison's hoarse wail still pulsed from the crib, but quieter now. She had cried herself out. Rosie could smell Gary's sweat and her own, and pee from the Diaper Genie and spit-up and stale baby powder.

"I can't do it no more," he said. "Her crying is in my head."

Rosie sank to the floor and cradled him to her.

Listening to Gary pack his things, Rosie's chest and throat ached like they did before a big cry, but she never did cry. Eventually that tight, can't-breathe feeling faded, but the doubts remained. What if she had fed Madison more? What if the house had a long hall so Gary could get away from the noise? What if it hadn't been so stifling hot—if the air conditioner had worked or Madison had been born in December instead of July? Maybe if the heat hadn't sapped him, Gary could have found more patience somewhere deep inside himself.

There wasn't any point in "what-iffing."

For five years now, Gary had been out of her and Madison's life, but also in it. Rosie walked a delicate line to keep it that way. She didn't press him to pay child support or nag about who he dated. She always had something savory on the stove when he came by and she kept her bedroom door open for him, most of the time. What they did was play house. It might not be a house of bricks like the one the third Little Pig built, but it wasn't a house of straw, either. It was a twig-house, shaky, but it kept the rain off, even if it wouldn't survive a high wind.

Chapter 27

Walter started in puppetry when television was still fun, when hometown stations used local acts to fill gaps between soap operas and news. He and his marionettes had two regular weekday gigs at WRAL Channel Five in Raleigh: five minutes for his weatherman puppet, Partley Cloudy, who always made the opposite prediction from the regular weatherman in the last few minutes of the news, and a full fifteen minutes on the *Uncle Lee Show*, a live children's hour where Lee Casterline dressed up like a ringmaster and entertained kids and their parents. Lee gave Walter free rein, so Walter had been performing classic fairy tales, with puppeteering help from his friend Alf, who did double duty as a clown on the *Uncle Lee Show*. They'd done "The Princess and the Pea," "Little Red Riding Hood," "The Frog Prince," and several others. The younger kids in the audience squirmed and made a lot of noise but the older kids and parents seemed to like it.

In the employee break room that also served as the station's dressing room and supply closet, Walter put the finishing touches on a swan marionette that converted to an ugly duckling with one flip, saving Walter from having to change controllers. He was pleased with this puppet. Over the weekend, Rosie's grandmother had brought Rosie to the Ginkgo Street house. Rosie was six, a beauty with fair curls and big blue eyes. Walter had let her flip the puppet from swan to duckling and back again, as many times as she wanted. Every time, she laughed with surprised delight as if she hadn't seen the trick before.

He heard music start up in the studio and Lee Casterline announcing, "It's time to march!" The kids would march in a circle around the studio for five minutes, led by Alf the clown twirling his bowler hat, and then it would be time for Walter and a sweaty Alf to go on.

The station manager, Bill Jacobson, came into the break room carrying a hand puppet, a fleece cowboy the station used when the afternoon cooking demonstration ended early. "Kevin is sick today. I need you to do the hand puppet at four twenty-five."

"I don't do hand puppets," Walter said, gluing a final feather on the swan. "Ask one of the interns." The cowboy puppet didn't have a regular puppeteer. Anyone could shove a hand up it, no skill or artistry required.

"I need you to do it, so do it. And another thing. I told Lee no more giving away fifteen minutes of his show to your marionettes. I've been getting calls. Parents say their kids are either bored or scared. Some lady told me you left Little Red Riding Hood in the wolf's stomach, instead of having a woodsman come save her. What was that about? Her little girl had nightmares."

"That's how the original story ends," Walter said.

"The kids also don't like the strings. They want puppets like the Muppets on *Sesame Street*, where you can't see how they're operated. By next week you need to switch your puppets over to hand puppets."

Walter couldn't believe Bill's ignorance. "You don't just

convert marionettes to hand puppets. It's an entirely different art form."

"Then make you some new ones, with foam and felt like this guy." He tossed the cowboy puppet toward Walter. "Soft. Kids don't like hard."

"I don't do hand puppets!" Walter said, exasperated. "I do marionettes and fairy tales. They're as much for adults as children."

"There's no future in fairy tales, Walter. Children's programming is where it's at. If you want to stay on the air at this station, make the change." With that, Bill left. Down the hall in the studio, the marching music slowed down.

Walter sat holding his swan, smelling the break room's old coffee and cigarette smoke. Rosie's grandmother had told Walter that weekend that she would need more child support, since Kiki had disappeared again and the grandmother was raising Rosie. And there was Jane, who wore high-water pants to school every day because she was growing faster than Walter and Ernestine could earn money for new clothing.

He went home between sets to a quiet house. From his closet, he pulled down the box that held Mr. Svoboda's marionettes. If he sold just one, he wouldn't need the television job.

He hadn't looked at them in a while. He had forgotten how beautiful they were.

He lifted Punch from his nest in the box. *Every culture got a Punch*, he remembered Mr. Svoboda saying. *Pulcinella, Polichinelle. For me he is* Kasparek *but nobody here know that name.*

Walter pinched tears from his eyes. What had he wanted from his puppets? What had he thought would happen? That he might perform for kings like Mr. Svoboda? That it would be his privilege to bring old tales to life with his wood and papier-mâché and paints? His own arrogance embarrassed him.

He had wanted to create perfect beauty, and he had come so close. But now it swung away from him, leagues opening up between him and it.

Back at the station at 4:25 that afternoon, he pulled the cowboy puppet over his hand, almost gagging with claustrophobia.

Chapter 28

The granting of a wish may or may not bring happiness.

Jane ran her hand over the leather of the recliner in the spacious media room of Cora's childhood home, her foot elevated on the foot rest. She could recline the chair and adjust foot height as needed, or ask the chair to give her a massage. By voice command, she could operate the seventy-inch smart television and watch anything she wanted. When he deposited her today, Pete had brought up several bottles of wine from the basement and placed a corkscrew within Jane's reach.

She could get used to this.

The media room was once Cora's playroom. Walter and Luciana had unveiled it on Cora's third birthday. By then Jane was too old for toys, but that didn't prevent her from feeling jealous. The room featured a near-professional quality puppet stage that Jane didn't care about, but also a life-size plush horse, a cotton candy maker, and a pinball machine. A real pinball machine, like you would find in an arcade. Cora couldn't even reach the controls. Jane had cried to Avril on the phone that night, "She can't tie her shoes yet and he bought her that! *I'm* the one who listened to 'Pinball Wizard' every day of ninth grade, not her!" Avril had made soothing, sympathetic noises.

Jane wondered if that pinball machine was still here somewhere. When she grew more used to her crutches, she might limp around and see if she could find it.

The house was quiet. She tried out the voice activation for the television. The menu popped up, with a large still shot of Walter and his puppet Zeno with Johnny Carson, from Walter's first appearance on *The Tonight Show*.

"More choices!" Jane ordered, to get off that screen. Suggested viewing options came up: a documentary about Gray Steed Puppets, *The Muppet Movie, Labyrinth, Being John Malkovich*. Every season of *Zeno and Friends* that Jane had suffered through when her sons were little. This was the down side of staying in a house maintained for puppeteers.

"Anything but puppets!" Jane shouted. The command took her back to the main menu with *The Tonight Show* still. Zeno grinned out at her, his fur the bluest of blues.

The Tonight Show appearance was a turning point for Walter, and for Jane and Ernestine. Jane took a calming breath, composing her next instruction. She pressed the massage button. The chair's artificial hands pounded her mid-back, nearly knocking the breath out of her.

Jane remembered her mother calling her to the table at the Ginkgo Street house when she was a teenager. Chili, the pot soaking in cold, greasy dishwater in the sink. Dirty dishes on every surface. Splats of food baked hard on the stove. Ernestine's housekeeping was slovenly. Jane pulled out her chair with a loud scrape and sat. She would rather be anywhere but here. Her chest hurt, the pent up anger at her ridiculous parents burning her from the inside out.

As usual, Ernestine had her puppet, Tino, on her hand. "How was Janey's day at school?" the puppet piped. Jane ignored him.

He cocked his yellow head. "Aww, Janey in a bad mood?

When I'm in a bad mood I hum to myself, like this." He started to hum "Yellow Submarine."

"Oh my Godddd. If you have something to say to me, say it without a prop."

"A *prop!*" Tino turned to Ernestine, indignant. "She called me a *prop!*"

"There, there," Ernestine said.

Tino turned back to Jane. "Are you on your period?"

"Oh my Godddd." Jane clutched her face.

Walter hadn't come when Ernestine called, but now he entered the kitchen carrying a hand puppet, made of foam and the same spiky synthetic fur as Tino, only this puppet was light blue.

On Ernestine's hand, Tino reared back in shock. The black pupils in his plastic eyes rattled. "Who have we here?"

Walter examined his puppet. "Anybody can make one of these. It took me a morning."

"Make it, maybe, but not bring it to life," Ernestine said. She had created her Tino years before Jane was born. She was always inventing new routines and jokes for Tino.

"Hand puppets," Walter scoffed.

Jane had heard her parents bicker for years about the relative merits of hand puppets versus marionettes. Their teasing had turned to contempt. She ladled chili into a bowl. A sheen of grease floated on the surface. Chunks of tofu drifted among the beans.

Walter served himself and ate a spoonful. He made a face.

Tino pursed his furry lips. "If Mr. Marionette man not like Ernestine's cooking, maybe he should cook for his own self."

Walter wiped his mouth and put the blue puppet on his hand. Its high voice was a cruel imitation of Tino. "If Ernestine can't manage to cook or clean, maybe she need to get a job."

Jane groaned. "Not you, too."

"Ernestine have a job," Tino said.

"A job that pays real money," the blue puppet said. "Puppet story time at library not pay the bills."

"Lazy marionette man also not pay bills." Tino shrugged. "Bills don't get paid."

"At least lazy marionette man not a fat cow," the blue puppet said.

Tears rose in Ernestine's eyes. "Fuck you," Tino said.

Walter laughed. "This thing's pretty handy." He held up the puppet, making it look this way and that.

Jane had had enough. She grabbed the blue puppet off Walter's hand. She ripped open the seam between its head and shoulder and flung it. It landed in the sink with a splash.

Tino clasped his yellow hands together. "My hero!"

"I hate you both!" The sour ache in Jane's chest spread to her throat. "You and your stupid puppets. When I turn eighteen I'm out of here and you'll never see me again."

Walter got up from the table. He lifted the limp blue puppet from the dishwater and wrung it out. A wooden spoon had lodged inside the puppet. He played with it, sticking the spoon handle up one of the puppet's arms. He wiggled it to make the puppet move. "I guess that's it," he said to no one but himself.

Jane left with a disgusted shriek, slamming out the front door into the dusk. She walked the neighborhood until late, in the hope that her parents would worry, but the house was dark and quiet when she returned.

Three months later, Walter was invited to appear on *The Tonight Show* with Johnny Carson. The scheduled act, Frank Oz, had laryngitis and couldn't appear with Miss Piggy, so he put in a good word for Walter. When Walter told Ernestine and Jane, Tino rose up on Ernestine's arm and said, "Miss Piggy must have a Kermit the Frog in her throat." Even Jane thought that one was pretty funny.

The Tonight Show was a huge break. At home in North Carolina, Jane and Ernestine, and Tino, stayed up to watch. Ernestine made popcorn. She passed the bowl to Jane with her Tino hand. "Does you want some popcorn?" Tino offered.

"No, thank you," Jane said, too excited about the show to remember to ignore Tino.

When the curtain parted for Walter's act, it wasn't the normal marionette rail with his fairy tale puppets and Walter playing God above. Instead, the blue puppet Jane had almost drowned sat in the chair next to Johnny Carson's desk, swinging furry legs. Jane couldn't see any strings.

Johnny Carson spoke to the blue puppet.

"Now, what is your name?"

"My name Zeno, what's yours?" the blue puppet said in Walter's falsetto voice.

Ernestine stopped crunching popcorn.

"What name did he say?" asked Tino.

Ernestine turned up the volume.

"Zeno flew all the way from North Carolina to be with us tonight, folks," Carson said to the live audience.

"And boy are my arms tired," Zeno said.

On Ernestine's arm Tino said, "Unoriginal!"

"We're glad to have you, Zeno. Thanks for filling in for Frank Oz at the last minute," Carson said.

"You're welcome," said Zeno. "I heard Miss Piggy had a Kermit the Frog in her throat." Laughter burst from the audience.

"What the fuck?" Ernestine struggled up from the couch to stand in front of the television. Tino slipped from her hand onto the floor.

"That's my joke. The bastard stole my puppet and my joke."

Jane picked Tino up. She held his lifeless body in her lap as Johnny Carson's live studio audience cheered.

Chapter 29

Cora dreamed of her father.

She was at Bevins, to make sure the staff had him exercise while Jane was out of commission. She went through a door to find him and found herself outside, near the edge of a cliff.

His back was to her. He held a puppet, a raven carved of holly, the wood stained dark, feathers of leather. And yet it wasn't a puppet. It had no strings, no rods, and when he lifted it over his head and let go, the raven flew off with a heavy beat of wings.

A younger, laughing Walter looked over his shoulder at Cora. His hair was dark and not receded. "Isn't he a beauty?" Walter opened his arms to the raven that had lighted on a tree. "Oh, magnificent fellow!"

"Dad, you look so much better than the last time I saw you!" Love swelled in Cora.

He had a spring in his step. He cupped her face. "Pumpkin!"

Around them, figures moved, his creations from the *Birdlandia* storyboard. Their sheer size made her nervous but Walter was ecstatic and she knew, as one does in a dream, that with him by her side nothing could harm her. Hulking beings of purple and emerald and brown lumbered around them, while small bird-like creatures lit on their backs, cracking jokes. She saw no cords, no hidden risers for the sets, no straining puppeteers gazing at monitors. The creatures moved on their own. All around was a scent of freshly cut grass that Cora never smelled in the city and had forgotten until this moment.

She awoke in her bed, disoriented. It had seemed so real. She reached for a notepad and began to sketch the raven.

She took her drawings to Olin. Instead of his retrofitting the mechanical skeleton, they would build this raven puppet together.

"Yes, I can do it," he said. "What movement do you want for the wings?"

She showed him with her hands. "And the neck should rotate, like this."

"And tilt. Ravens cock their heads."

"Yes, do that."

"What fairy tales will you tell with it? Will I see it on Jimmy Fallon or Broadway?"

After Walter had shot down her idea for a *Tangled Tales* pilot, Cora had only brought it up with him one other time, when she took him to see *Wicked* on Broadway for his birthday. "It's an alternative fairy tale," she pointed out. "They're making money at it."

"Now you just seem unoriginal," he said.

"It's for me," she told Olin, and he nodded. He placed her sketches on a lathe and anchored them with one of his metal stars. He turned the shop's "Open" sign to "Closed" and lowered the bay door.

AFTERWARD, THEY LAY ON A BLANKET ON HIS SHOP FLOOR. Sunlight from high windows cast perfect wall-shadow and without thinking, Cora formed a wolf puppet with her fingers, then a rabbit.

Olin traced the dip of her collarbone with his finger. "When did you know you wanted to be a puppeteer?"

"By high school, I guess."

She and her father had created shadow puppets for a sequence he wanted to try on the *Zeno and Friends* television show to differentiate Zeno's imagination. Walter spent more time in New York than Raleigh during Cora's high school years, but he came home for her junior year spring break. Heads together in Cora's old playroom, they used X-ACTO knives to cut out Zeno, an elephant and monkey, a smiling moon, and trailing willow trees for props. In person the puppets were grotesque: oversized and gangly, cardboard limbs marred with pen marks and duct tape, grommets and brass brads showing at the hinges. But when Walter and Cora pressed them to a homemade back-lit screen, their tiny shadows made magic.

"Everything is prettier in shadow," he said.

Cora taped chopstick control rods to the back of the monkey. Her mother swept in, wearing tennis whites from a morning at the country club, her favorite diamond bracelet glittering on her tanned wrist. Around her swirled the expensive Chanel she preferred for days when she planned to perspire. She waved an envelope. "Cora, darling, we did it! Look what came in the mail!"

Cora tested the monkey's movements on the makeshift screen. Heat from the halogen lamp seared her face. "What is it?"

"It's your invitation to the Royal Laurel Brigade of Guards ball!"

Classmates at Cora's private school talked incessantly about debutante parties, but Cora hadn't paid much attention.

Walter fastened alligator clips to Zeno's rods. "I told you I didn't want us doing that social climbing shit," he said.

"And I ignored you," Luciana said. "This will be so much fun, Cora. The parties! The dresses!"

Cora glanced at the invitation. "I can't. It's the same weekend as the Puppeteers of America conference." This year, a Vietnamese troupe would perform water puppetry, and she could take workshops in street creatures and playwriting.

"This is more important. It's your chance to meet the right class of people. Those bohemians your father hangs out with are nice enough but they aren't husband material. The father of my grandchildren can't be a penniless puppeteer."

"I don't want kids. I want puppets." Cora curled the monkey's arm to scratch its head. "Look at this cutie."

"Genes like yours should be passed on, darling."

"I want to be a puppeteer." Cora hadn't said those words aloud before. Her father looked up.

"Puppeteers are grown-ups who never stopped playing with toys," Luciana scoffed.

"My toys pay for your shopping habit," Walter said.

"Damn it, Walter, Cora's social life is my domain," Luciana said. "I worked hard to get this invitation. Smiled until my face froze, broke nails volunteering for the chair's favorite charity, donated thousands of dollars—"

"Of my money," Walter cut her off. "Cora, you don't have to do the debutante thing if you don't want to."

"Cora," her mother pleaded.

Cora imagined potential alliances in an electrified triangle. She and her mother in white dresses at the ball. She and her father ring-mastering a shadow circus. A broken hypotenuse between her parents. "I want to be a puppeteer," she said.

Luciana stormed out in a huff.

Walter adjusted the brads on Zeno's knee joints. "Are you sure you want to be a puppeteer? There are easier choices."

Cora took the smiling cutout moon and raised it in the sky behind willow tendrils.

Walter reared back Zeno's head to admire the moon. "Aahhh." Every spike of Zeno's fur and every willow leaf appeared sharp in black-and-white behind the screen.

"I'm sure," Cora said.

Now, lying beside her in the shop, Olin said, "Puppetry seems like an odd career choice for a teenager."

"I'm not sure it was really a choice. Someone had to carry on the family name. And I love it, the puppetry. The business side, not so much." Cora stretched and sat up, reaching for her clothes.

"You're always leaving," he said.

She kissed him. "It's Friday. I meet with Alice on Fridays."

He grasped her ankle then let go. "Come see me another day of the week."

CORA SET UP HER FRIDAY SUNSET PERFORMANCE FOR ALICE IN the conference room.

It was early yet but Alice came in with her little girl, Dee, a second grader. Dee worked a sock puppet.

"Childcare fail," Alice said. "Barbara's at a conference and the nanny has pink eye. Can Dee stay here while I take the call from Disney about your dad's film?"

"That's today? Fingers crossed. Dee, you can watch my new version of 'Diamonds and Toads.' See if you like it."

Dee took Alice's usual chair. Cora readied the string of beads that would allow her kind-daughter puppet to spew precious stones without requiring Cora's second hand. She placed a black fur hat on her servant puppet to convert it from pitiful crone to a male character. She was enthralled with the silent facility of the new ring mechanism. By comparison, her kind-daughter puppet seemed creaky and primitive. She would need to take all her puppets to Olin.

The thought of Olin made her face grow warm.

Dee smoothed the yarn hair of the sock puppet on her hand.

"Do you want to be a puppeteer when you grow up?" Cora asked.

Dee shrugged. "Maybe. I might want to be a kindergarten teacher."

Girls should be allowed to be whatever they want to be, Cora thought. She began her fairy tale.

In her forties now, the sister whom the Fairy had blessed with the utterance of jewels and flowers visited a Reverser of Curses.

"It's just so tedious," she explained, removing a pearl from her tongue and flicking it away as if it were a bitter lemon seed. "Twenty years of vomiting precious stones, countless chipped teeth. And on top of that the corporate worries now that we've

taken the chain national. Cut-throat competition with Helzberg and Jared. Budgets and ad-buys and hiring problems that my husband, Prince Harold, won't let us delegate."

As she spoke, four large diamonds, a ruby, and a rose dropped from her mouth. She caught them expertly in a golden spittoon. She selected the ruby and placed it on the table between her and the Reverser of Curses. "This should cover your fee."

His hands twitched but he didn't yet accept it. "Surely you're grateful," he said. "You have riches beyond measure, and the satisfaction of knowing that your wealth sprang from your kindness."

"Kindness," she scoffed. "What kindness? The Fairy caught me on a good day and I minded my manners. My sister had menstrual cramps when it was her turn. Now I watch her and her husband, Pete, running their bait and tackle shop at the lake, so happy. This year they opened a little cafe in the back, specializing in frog legs. Pete adores her and in October they board the place up and take their pop-up camper to Florida. I haven't had a vacation in years."

With her agitation, jewels struck the spittoon with the sound of hail on a tin roof. She picked up a daffodil, bruised from the crush of tanzanites and garnets, and held it to her chin. "T'would have been better if the Fairy had blessed me with flowers only. I could have opened a florist shop next to my sister, supplied edible nasturtiums to top wedding cakes. Married a man who loved me for me." She burped up an especially large diamond and examined it for flaws. "So, can you help me?"

"Alas, I can only reverse curses, not blessings, though I grant you it can be hard to tell the difference at times. These things have two sides, and the side one sees has more to do with the seer than the seen."

"You're implying I should change my attitude," she said. "Be more grateful and optimistic. You sound like Harold. And my mother, who insists on living with us, by the way. If that's not a curse I don't know what is. Is there truly nothing you can do?"

The Reverser of Curses eyed her overflowing bowl of jewels. "I'm afraid not."

"Then refer me to a practitioner who will reverse a blessing. I can pay any cost."

"Any cost? Madam, think what you are saying. You do not want to consort with such folk. Theirs is dark magic indeed."

"So I'm stuck." She coughed pearls into her hand as if spitting gristle into a napkin.

"Try not to think of it as stuck. Return home. Give thanks for what you have. Perhaps move your mother out of the house. Take a class in flower arranging to satisfy your creative side." With visible regret, he pushed the ruby toward her.

"Keep it," she said with a sigh.

"What do you think?" Cora asked Dee.

Dee swiveled in Alice's chair. "I like the regular way better."

At that moment, Alice came back. She closed the door behind her. She had an odd look on her face.

"Do they want the film?" Cora asked.

"They want Gray Steed Puppets," Alice said.

Chapter 30

Rosie was about tired of this diet. She'd lost eight pounds, then last week gained most of it back. Today she blew off the weigh-in and marched down the clinic's shiny white hallway to Nelson's office. In her hand she gripped the mason jar she'd brought to help make her point.

Nelson sat at his desk, on the phone. She could tell by his smile and the tease in his voice he was talking to a girl. When he saw Rosie he said, "I got to go, baby," and hung up.

Rosie lowered herself into a chair. "Don't let me interrupt."

"It's no problem."

"Was that your girlfriend?"

"That's a personal question." Nelson's cologne smelled like citrus fruit. His crisp white lab coat flattered his brown skin, and every tiny coil of hair held its place along his straight hairline. She bet he'd make some girl a good boyfriend.

"I just wondered," she said. "If I don't ask, how am I supposed to find out about people?"

Nelson rubbed his jaw. "Yes, it was my girlfriend."

"What's her name?"

"Jacqueline."

"That's a pretty name. You should have her picture in your office. It'd make it feel more homey in here."

"Thanks for the suggestion." He pulled up her food diary on his computer. "Looks like you're doing pretty well following the meal plan."

"I am but it's not working. All this time without anything that tastes good and I'm as fat as ever."

"You lost eight last time. Are you sure you're staying on the program?"

"Yes," she said, though she had eaten a couple little things she hadn't listed in her diary. Nothing big . . . just a half a Krispy Kreme Madison had left out on the counter—Rosie didn't want it to go to waste—and some fried chicken at a cousin's house so she wouldn't seem rude turning it down. And the slaw and mashed potatoes that went with the chicken. It was hard to eat chicken without sides. Taping up her fridge didn't help when the food people pushed at her wasn't inside the fridge.

"Well, it hasn't been all that long since you got serious about your diet. Give it time."

"It's felt like a long time to me. I can't focus on anything because I'm too busy thinking about how hungry I am. I've never been snappish but this diet has made me so I'm ill at everybody." Just last night she'd yelled at Madison and made her cry, for no reason other than dawdling at bedtime. Rosie had always thought she was a good person. Come to find out she was only as kind as the last piece of food she'd swallowed. She disappointed herself.

"If you stick with it—really stick with it—you'll start to see results soon, I promise."

Rosie brought out the mason jar and set it down under Nelson's nose. She'd filled the jar that morning with her best gravy, without taking so much as a taste for herself. "I know you're healthy and all, but if you stick your pinky finger in that it'll help you understand people like me better."

"I've had gravy before," he said.

"You haven't had *my* gravy."

He twisted the lid off, stuck a finger in and put it in his mouth. A look of bliss melted across his face.

"See what I mean?" she said. "It's good on egg noodles, right by itself without any actual meat. Or on white bread. Sometimes when I feel lazy at night I just heat it up and pour it over a piece of Sarah Lee white bread for Madison, let her eat it with a fork."

Nelson looked pained. "It's so bad for you, Rosie."

She reached out. "You want me to take it back?"

"No." He clutched the jar.

"All right then."

"I know it's hard to give this up completely. How about just cutting back? A teaspoon instead of half a cup."

"A teaspoon won't hardly even moisten one biscuit."

"A tablespoon, then. And no more than one biscuit. A small one."

Why did it have to be so hard? With so much at stake her brain ought to be able to tell her hand, *"Don't you put that in your mouth"* and her hand be like, *"Oh, yeah, you're right, my bad."* But it was so much more complicated than that.

"Will you keep trying?" Nelson asked her.

She sighed. "I guess so."

"You can do it, Rosie. I have faith in you. See you next week."

꙳

BACK AT HOME AFTER PICKING MADISON UP FROM KINDERGAR-
ten, Rosie made Madison a pimento cheese sandwich and
sent her outside to play. Without enthusiasm, she ate the
salad she'd prepared for herself.

Her kitchen looked like a bomb had gone off at a college fair.
To shore up the pennants, she'd started ordering college
brochures. There was a certain order to the postcards and
slick booklets that arrived daily. First, mailings addressed
to Madison with pictures of students having fun. Then one
to "the parents of Madison" with financial aid information.
Then they invited Madison to a campus sleepover, sending
mascot stickers that Rosie let Madison stick to her bedroom
door. Rosie felt a little guilty to be costing the colleges so
much in postage, when she was just using them to keep herself from eating between meals. She'd strung twine across
her kitchen and clothes-pinned the brochures to that, forming another barrier between her and food. She had to duck
under it and bat the brochures away to get to the refrigerator. It looked a little crazy but it was effective, sort of. And
harmless, until the phone call came.

"May I speak to Madison Calhoun?" a man's voice asked.

The mama bear in Rosie reared up. Why was a grown
man calling her kindergartener? "This is her mother. Who's
this?"

"Mrs. Calhoun, so nice to speak to you. My name is
Decker Byrne. I'm an admissions counselor at Ballard College. Madison has expressed interest in our school and I'm
calling to see if I can answer any questions for her."

Rosie's face went warm. It hadn't occurred to her that any of the schools might follow up in person.

"Is Madison available?" Decker Byrne said.

"She's not here right now," Rosie said. It was technically true. Madison was out on the porch playing with her Littlest Pet Shop bobbleheads.

"Kids these days, so many activities. What extracurriculars is Madison involved in?"

Rosie hesitated. She could answer in the present, and tell him playdates, Play-Doh, climbing trees, dance parties with stuffed animals. Or she could flat-out lie, selecting interests for Future Madison: debate club or swim team or Future Farmers of America, if schools still had that. She took the middle ground and extrapolated. "She dances," she blurted out. "It's her passion." The deception made her wince but she had to say something to get the man off the phone.

"That's fantastic," he said. "Ballard has a great dance program, and dancers can minor in business. It increases their chances of becoming employed within six months of graduation."

"That's good," Rosie said.

"I'll send Madison information on the dance department. If she wants to major in it, auditions start next month, but she can also take dance classes as electives if she decides to choose another major."

"Thanks," Rosie said. Madison might enjoy dancing for fun without the pressure of maintaining a ballerina body.

"If you don't mind me asking, what other schools is Madison considering?"

Rosie looked at the pennants on her fridge. "NC State, Clemson, Meredith, UNC Chapel Hill, University of Hawaii." That last one had been an indulgence, ordered on a cold, wet day when Rosie longed for sun and sand and tropical flowers. She hadn't mentioned it to Madison, who got anxious at the thought of going to college far from home.

"All good schools, though we'd like the opportunity to show how Ballard might be the best fit. Are any of those your alma mater, or your husband's?"

"Neither me nor Madison's daddy went to college," Rosie said. "But Madison's a lot smarter than us."

"I'm sure you're plenty smart, Mrs. Calhoun. We have a special program for students who are the first in their family to go to college, with tutoring services and financial counseling for parents. I'll send you information. Is there anything else I can answer for you at this time?"

"I don't think so," Rosie said.

"Well, don't hesitate to reach out if you or Madison have questions."

When he hung up Rosie sat for a minute, feeling pleasure in the aftermath of his warm, welcoming voice.

Ordering the college brochures had put Madison on all kinds of mailing lists, for things like SAT prep courses, summer abroad programs, Army recruitment. In today's mail, a large postcard from Jostens reminded Madison to order her graduation gown and mementos.

Rosie got online. If she was shopping, she wasn't eating. The Jostens website asked for Madison's school. Rosie typed in "homeschooled." She ordered a graduation gown, a mortar board, and tassel. She could hem the gown. She looked at the class rings. Madison would love a ring. Rosie couldn't afford it, but she added it to her cart anyway. Why not? She had twelve years to find the money.

She looked at the graduation invitations. The traditional embossed kind, or the modern design with the graduate's smiling photograph? Madison would graduate kindergarten in a few weeks. A party would be fun. Rosie could invite her sisters, and Ernestine, and Gary and his brother. Kiki and Walter probably couldn't come but she would invite them anyway, since the invitations came twenty-five to a box.

The conversation with Decker Byrne had brought Madison's future into sharp focus. Madison could grow up and go to college, get a good job, marry someone educated, have smart children. That future seemed real enough to taste, if Rosie could manage to choose it over fats and carbs.

Chapter 31

By day three, the allure of the MacArthur Downs mansion was wearing thin. Jane had explored the entire main level without finding the pinball machine or anything else at all personal. The house was sterile, like a hotel. Maybe there were more interesting things in the basement, but she wasn't going to risk a fall by trying the stairs.

She killed an hour making phone calls for work, but there was only so much she could do without going to the office. Jane was bored. And lonely. And her stupid foot hurt. When Pete rang the doorbell and let himself in with a "Yoo-hoo!" she teared up with gratitude and had to swipe her eyes with the sleeve of her borrowed Egyptian cotton bathrobe before he entered the living room.

"How's the foot?" He set a cardboard box and a vase of grocery store roses on the coffee table. "Brought you flowers."

"Thanks." On her first date with Pete, a walk around his neighborhood, they had passed a cemetery and he had joked, "If I ever bring you flowers you'll know where I got them." She wondered if he remembered that.

"The foot's okay. I should be able to put weight on it after my next doctor visit."

"What about driving?"

"Not until the damn boot comes off."

"I can drive you," he offered.

"I'll Uber."

"Don't do that. I'm just down the road. I'll take you wherever."

She shrugged. "Okay. I'll let you know."

Pete opened the cardboard box. "I brought your home movies. There are some cute shots of you and Rosie."

"Really?" Jane hadn't expected footage of anything but puppet shows.

"I made duplicates for Rosie and Cora, no charge."

Pete was sweet. Irresponsible, but sweet. "Thanks," she said.

He looked around. "Have you got everything you need? Enjoying life at the big house?"

"I'm bored."

"How about I come back tonight? I'll bring takeout. China Palace. You like that."

"I don't know . . ."

"Oh, come on. We can play Scrabble."

Now that was tempting. She always beat him at Scrabble. He got tied up forming long, fancy words while she racked up points on "cat." They were divorced. They should act like they were divorced, arm's length, but Jane was starved for company. "Okay, come on by," she said.

After Pete left, she flipped through the jewel cases in the cardboard box. Pete had labeled the DVDs as best he could, based on what he saw on the film. She picked one at random, "*Uncle Lee Show*; Easter" and hobbled to the DVD player. At least watching Walter's movies would give her something to do.

She recognized the set of the *Uncle Lee Show* immediately. She used to go with Walter to the TV station. On screen, in faded color, Uncle Lee called out, "It's time to march!" Children walked in a circle around the studio in time to the music Uncle Lee banged out on the piano. Walter's friend Alf Anderson, dressed as a clown, twirled his bowler hat. Jane looked but didn't find herself among the marchers. The camera cut to a marionette bridge at the edge of the set and zoomed in. The curtain opened and her father's marionette dog stepped out and began doing tricks. The dog galloped across the stage, stopped, and scratched its ear with a hind leg. That particular puppet had a mouth string. When it dropped its jaw its little red tongue stuck out. Jane could hear children laughing and smiled in spite of herself. Her father really was a master manipulator, as they said in the trade.

The next scene was the backyard at Ginkgo Street, in bright sunshine. A puppet stage was set up near the scraggly garden, but the camera wasn't focused on it. Instead, Jane watched her teenage self help Rosie find Easter eggs. Rosie had blonde curls that later darkened and relaxed. Rosie's grandmother had dressed her in a frilly white dress with blue satin sash. Jane's hair was cut in wings. Avril had cut it for her. She was barefoot, wearing a pair of gray Levi cords she remembered buying with her babysitting money. What struck Jane was that her dad was filming her and Rosie. It wasn't that they had wandered into the frame as his camera on a tripod filmed his marionettes. He was looking at *them* through the viewfinder.

Rosie ran toward the camera until her face filled the screen. The camera shook. "Whoa, girl, you're gonna knock me over!"

Jane hadn't realized how much she missed hearing her father's voice speaking coherent words. Her throat caught.

Walter's left hand worked his gypsy princess marionette while his right held the camera. He often toyed with that puppet when he was working out some problem. Sometimes when the puppet wasn't handy, his left hand unconsciously made her movements. He held the control out of Rosie's reach and the princess curtsied to Rosie.

"Jane! Come over here!" Her dad called. Jane couldn't make out her reply. Walter turned the camera on her.

"Don't film me!" The young Jane had a baby face, plump cheeks. Where had those gone?

Rosie ran to Jane and hugged her legs. Jane crouched and pointed, showing Rosie a plastic egg hidden under a plant. Rosie ran out of the frame but the camera stayed on Jane. Sunlight brought out the auburn in her hair. From her crouch she fell backward on her hands, then pushed up into a backbend, her T-shirt riding up to show a flat stomach. Rosie ran over and tickled her until she collapsed, laughing, the camera never leaving her.

Jane hit the power button and sat in silence. She had no memory of that day. Why did she only cultivate resentful memories, not beautiful days like that one?

Chapter 32

Cora searched the Gray Steed archives for her father's marionettes to lend to the Smithsonian. She had seen them when she hunted for the *Birdlandia* storyboards, packed away in the same beat-up cases he'd used before he made it big. He had the packing for his shows down pat, each case just under fifty pounds to avoid excess baggage charges when he flew.

She opened the first case. These were Walter's own pieces, not his valuable Czech marionettes, which were on display under locked UV-protective glass in the Gray Steed lobby. He had carved some puppets from poplar and white pine, made others from papier-mâché. The smell alone made her happy: the slight chemical odor of paint, tape, aging flour. He had stopped performing these puppets in public before Cora was born, but they were the characters he taught her with. She remembered watching these little people come to life on the floor, heads cocking and shoulders shrugging, so lifelike she forgot that her father was controlling them.

She lifted the soldier with the tinderbox from the case. She remembered her father telling her about a trip to Czechoslovakia in the 1980s, when he was invited to try out the marionettes at the Czech National Marionette Theatre, and as soon as he picked up one particular knight he could tell that his own Mr. Svoboda had made it. There was something in the weight and balance that put his friend right there in the room. If someone had blindfolded Cora and handed her one of her father's marionettes she would have recognized him as the maker. Walter was there, in the heft of head and limbs, the taut and slack dance of strings under the controls.

She gave the soldier a nostalgic kiss. Walter had showed her how to make the soldier move in a pendulum swing, landing with one rakish boot tucked behind the other. The airplane control had a detachable leg bar that allowed the puppeteer to pull the puppet in the direction he would walk. The boots were heavy oak to help keep them on the floor instead of floating.

Next was the frog prince, with long jointed legs made of layered masking tape painted green. A sticky red tongue lolled from his wide mouth. Underneath it were Rosie's ugly duckling and the gypsy princess marionette Walter was leaving to Jane. Their strings were slightly entangled and Cora gently freed them. Because of the marionettes, Cora could untangle anything. It was her superpower, the ability to see how a necklace chain or shoestring had become knotted. "The worst thing you can do is drop the control on the floor," Walter had taught her early on. "But if you do, separate the strings like so. Marionettes *want* to untangle. We hang them so they'll spin and flip back into place."

He was patient with her. She only remembered him losing his temper once. She had started to make the frog prince and his princess hug. "No, no, no! *Never* let two marionettes hug! You'll never get them apart!" He grabbed the controls from her, separating, untwisting. Cora had observed him through slitted eyes. The next day, she made two glove puppets, a Jack and Jill who could hug each other as hard and long as they, or she, wished.

She lay the frog prince beside the soldier. It wasn't entirely true that marionettes couldn't hug. One could do it, tip the controls in opposition to each other, choreograph and time it, preferably with two puppeteers. It was possible: her father simply wasn't willing to put in the effort. She didn't care to think about the metaphor.

Cora took photos of the marionettes, the props and pieces of stage, to email to the Smithsonian. Someone knocked on the open door. The receptionist stood there with Olin. "Olin Babich to see you?"

It disconcerted Cora to see him here. She went to his world. He didn't come to hers. It was as if he had stepped over a frontier wearing seven-league boots.

"Is it okay?" the receptionist asked.

"Yes, of course. Thank you."

The receptionist left. Olin ducked his head to enter.

"Hi!" Cora said.

He came closer. "These your father's puppets?" He looked thinner than she remembered, his faded jeans looser around the hips.

"Yes."

"They're all marionettes."

"His first love."

He touched the soldier puppet. "Beautiful. Why did he go from these to Zeno? More money, I guess."

"Not just money." Walter had always been sensitive to the suggestion that he had sold out. "I have a theory. He named his puppet Zeno. Zeno's paradox says that if you want to cross a room, first you have to cover half the distance. Then, you have to cover half the remaining distance. Then half the remaining distance again. You can never get to the other side of the room."

"And that relates to puppets how?"

"It has to do with the quest for perfection in art. I know artists who've quit when they couldn't achieve it. When I perform my puppets, I can never achieve the perfect merge of language and movement, but getting as close as the laws of physics allow exhilarates me. For my dad, the near miss was painful, I think. His reaction to the frustration was to give up."

"Or it coulda been the money," Olin teased.

He was close enough now that their arms touched. "What are you doing here, anyway?" she said.

He gestured around the small room, the puppets lying in state. "Am I not welcome here, in your little kingdom?"

"I didn't mean that. I just wasn't expecting you."

He unslung a gym bag from his shoulder. "I have your raven." He opened the bag and unwrapped cotton bunting. The raven looked up at her, black eyes bright and watchful, leather feathers. She fit it over her hand, breathing out an enthralled "Ohhh."

"I added a ball joint, so you can cock the head sideways as well as up and down. If you don't like it I can change it."

"It's fabulous." She imagined the gestures she could accomplish. "Perfect."

"I won't have a hostage anymore."

"What?" She was absorbed in trying out the puppet. It was magical. Like holding a live bird in her hand.

The Puppeteer's Daughters

"You'll have to come back of your own free will."

She met his eyes. His tone was sardonic but his hands hung loose and empty at his side. He was steeling himself for the possibility that she wouldn't return. Would she?

She owed it to him to be honest. "Something's happened. A chance for me to get free from Gray Steed Puppets and do my own art. And while I'm extricating myself from one thing, it might be best if I didn't entangle myself in another." Where was this speech coming from? Why would she even consider passing on this man? "I'm flying to Raleigh today to check on my father while my sister is laid up, and to think things over."

He leaned in and kissed her, his lips hovering over hers. "I'm not an entanglement. You can have both: me, and whatever this thing is you want."

She set the raven aside and pressed her hand to the back of Olin's neck to bend him toward her. She kissed him, the smell of his skin lighting every nerve. His upper arms were hard as tree limbs. Where was the softness of Olin Babich? In his lips.

He straightened up. "You know where I am when you're ready." She could tell he wanted to ask her if she would be back, but he wouldn't beg. And she wouldn't promise.

With a wave he was gone. Cora leaned on the table. Her father's gypsy princess looked up at her with an expression that said Cora was nuts for letting Olin go.

CORA ROLLED HER SUITCASE THROUGH THE FRONT DOORS OF Gray Steed Puppets to head to the airport. On the sidewalk,

Sabine and Madame Bea were entertaining a tourist couple whose sleepy toddler was strapped in a stroller. Cora stopped to indulge in the show.

"Do you remember when you found me?" Madame Bea said to Sabine, like a child asking for a story she had heard many times before.

"Of course I remember. I saw your foot peeking from a trashcan in the park. When I investigated, I found you. Your strings were so tangled."

"There is no worse feeling than tangled strings." Madame Bea shook her turbaned head. "You untangled me."

"It took a while," Sabine said. "I unknotted your knots. I untwisted your twists. When I was done I held your control in the air and you danced on the ground!"

Madame Bea did a little tap dance to demonstrate. The child in the stroller watched, wide-eyed. Cora found herself smiling.

"Tell about my eye," Madame Bea said.

Sabine clucked her tongue. "You were in bad shape. Some naughty child had gouged your eye and ripped out your hair."

"You made me an eye patch and covered my hair." Madame Bea's wooden hand touched her red eye patch. "Thank you." Madame Bea began to dance again, her legs moving while her upper body held still. Sabine deftly manipulated the puppet with one hand and used the other to pass her Styrofoam tip cup to the tourists. The man stuffed a ten dollar bill in the cup and the family left, smiling.

Sabine and Madame Bea shuffled toward Cora.

"I've never seen you two without your umbrella cart," Cora said.

"We like a sunny day as well as a wet one," Sabine said.

Madame Bea laid her hand on Cora's suitcase. "I predict that you will take a trip."

Cora laughed out loud. She reached in her purse and handed Sabine a twenty. "However do you do it, Madame Bea?"

"I see what I see," Madame Bea said. "Have you found your giant?"

The question brought Cora up short. She looked from the marionette to Sabine. The old woman's filmy eyes twinkled.

Cora swallowed. "I'm not sure."

"What about the other loved one?" Madame Bea asked.

Cora wasn't comfortable divulging information to Sabine and Madame Bea. They seemed to know too much about her already. "No progress," she said.

Madame Bea's head lolled sorrowfully. "I do not think you will find her. I see her lost. Far from home."

"Or she doesn't exist," Cora said, feeling sorrow of her own. She spotted a taxi and stuck her arm out to hail it. It pulled to the curb. The driver jumped out and loaded her suitcase in the trunk. Cora climbed in the cab. "LaGuardia," she told the driver.

As she closed the door, Madame Bea called after her, arms flailing. "I see what I see! There *is* another one!"

Chapter 33

Rosie waited in her car in the driveway of the MacArthur Downs house until Cora's cab drove up. It was cowardice, but she didn't feel like facing a cabin-feverish Jane alone today. Once Cora got out of the taxi with her luggage, Rosie hefted the basket of food she'd cooked to replenish Jane's supply. The basket held fried chicken, a full pan of macaroni and cheese, green beans flavored with ham hock, and an apple pie, and she hadn't even taken a single taste as she cooked. Somebody ought to give her a medal. Maybe she'd order herself one.

She met Cora on the porch.

"You ready for this?" Cora unlocked the door. A metal star hung on a leather string around her neck. Cora rarely wore jewelry. There was something appealing about the star's flecked surface and its uneven points.

"That's pretty," Rosie said.

Cora touched her throat. "Oh, thanks."

They went inside.

Jane yelled from the media room. "I'm in here!"

Cora cut Rosie a look. They braced themselves and went in. Jane reclined with her foot elevated, a box of DVDs and thumb drives spilling its contents at her feet. She paused whatever she'd been watching and smiled at them, in a much better mood than when Rosie last visited.

Rosie showed her the food. "I'll just pop this in the fridge and you can eat it whenever."

"How are you?" Cora asked. "Do you need anything? Want a pillow under that foot?"

"It's come to this," Jane said. "I used to babysit Rosie, Rosie babysat you, and now you two are babysitting me."

"We were more than each other's babysitters," Rosie said. "Right?"

"How's Dad?" Cora asked.

"Not great," Jane said. "They say he's speaking less, and he hasn't been eating well since his escape attempt. He might have had a small stroke, but there's no point taking him for a CT scan since they can't do anything about it if it was a stroke. I need to get over to Bevins."

"I'll go by on my way home, maybe take him a little of the mac and cheese," Rosie said. She hoped Jane didn't blame her for Walter's decline.

Cora picked up a VHS tape from the cardboard box and turned it over. "What's all this?"

"I'll show you." Jane pointed the remote at the TV as if casting a spell.

It took a moment for Rosie to realize what she was seeing, first folds of red cloth, and then a little stick puppet with a fishing-cork head parting the curtain. The frame pulled back. It was the *Amahl and the Night Visitors* puppet stage from their childhood Christmases, hanging above the basement stairs at Ginkgo Street. Faint in the background came the opera's opening oboe strains, music she hadn't heard in years.

A head of blonde curls poked out from behind the stage curtain. "Look, Daddy!"

"That's me!" Rosie said.

"Cute," Cora said.

Cora didn't understand. There were probably a thousand home videos of Cora. Rosie had never seen her child self on film. She watched as young Rosie waved from the minaret-shaped stage opening, a blue-eyed giant. "I see you!"

A voice, Jane's, spoke patiently. "Don't let them see you."

Child Rosie was holding the King Kaspar puppet.

"It's not time for Kaspar yet," Jane's voice said. "Be Amahl."

Rosie's small hand took the shepherd boy puppet. "What do I say?"

"Nothing. Act out what the music says." On the record album, Amahl's mother accused him of making up fairy tales. Jane's stick puppet of Amahl's mother shook a scolding finger at Amahl.

Child Rosie was still holding King Kaspar, but not tightly enough. Kaspar dived off the edge of the stage onto the floor as if committing suicide.

"Kaspar!"

Walter's arm reached out from where he was filming. It picked Kaspar up and held it for Rosie to grab. "Here, sweetheart."

Rosie remembered that Amahl performance, how excited she was to be behind the stage for the first time instead of in the audience, but she didn't remember her father saying *sweetheart*. She had never noticed Walter's camera aimed at her, only at his own performances. When he filmed, Rosie had felt sorry for his puppets because he looked away from them, only interested in how his monitor created a stage for their flipped images.

"There are a lot of you from Ginkgo Street, Rosie," Jane said. "And me."

On film, puppets twirled on their sticks, robes flying out like parasols. Walter's deep laughter drowned out the music and made the camera shake.

"Listen to him laugh," Cora said.

"I used to think every family acted out *Amahl* with stick puppets at Christmastime," Rosie said. "The first Christmas me and Gary were together I told him we should do *Amahl* and he thought I was talking about a shopping mall."

"We were not every family." Jane paused the video. "Ma had these. I haven't even scratched the surface. Pete made you both a set."

"I wonder where those puppets got to," Cora said. "I remember the shoebox we kept them in. They might be here. I can check the basement."

"I'll come with you," Rosie offered.

"Me, too." Jane struggled up and reached for her crutches.

"Jane, you can't do the basement stairs with your foot in a boot," Cora said.

"Just watch me. I need a fucking activity."

"You are such a bad patient," said Cora.

Rosie went down the steps first, to cushion Jane if she fell. Cora brought up the rear. Jane made it down the steps, breathing hard.

The MacArthur Downs basement was clean and well organized. Toward the front were utility shelves with tools, leftover paint, cleaning supplies. A humming wine cooler held a nice collection of wines, somewhat depleted by Pete bringing bottles up for Jane. In a back corner were personal things.

Cora lifted a dust cover, revealing her childhood puppet stage and the pinball machine.

Jane made an "ooooh" sound and laid a reverent hand on the pinball machine.

"I need to donate some of this stuff," Cora said.

"Donate the pinball machine to me," Jane said.

"What will you do with it?" Cora asked.

"I will *have* it," Jane said.

Cora shrugged. "Okay. I'll let the management company know." She searched a shelf of boxes and plastic bins and stood on her tiptoes to reach a shoebox. "I knew I'd seen this." She brushed a spider off the top and opened it.

The *Amahl* puppets were somewhat the worse for wear since Rosie had last seen them. Melchior's Styrofoam head rolled around in the bottom of the box, Amahl's mother was missing an eye, the cotton of Balthazar's beard was pulled thin. Still, it was like seeing old friends.

"I remember when Dad and I made these." Jane found Kaspar and straightened his gold braid crown. She handed him to Rosie. "You can finally have Kaspar."

Rosie cradled the puppet. She remembered sitting on Jane's lap on the backstage stairs, holding up all three kings while, on the LP, the kings sang their thanks to Amahl's mother for hosting them. Later, Jane and Rosie taught Cora. Amahl was Christmas Eve. Warmth, the illusion of family.

She wanted to take Kaspar home, but it didn't feel right

to separate the three kings. "I'll leave him with the others for now."

Cora handed Melchior to Jane and kept Balthazar for herself. "Hold them up," she said, taking out her phone for a selfie. She showed the photo to Rosie and Jane, the three of them smiling in the basement's artificial light, the three kings with their pushpin mouths looking perpetually surprised.

Cora posted to Instagram, typing a caption. "The Puppeteer's Daughters."

"Great," Jane said. "Now help me back up the stairs."

Chapter 34

After they deposited Jane safely back in her recliner, Rosie left to visit Walter, and Cora took the MacArthur Downs SUV to pick up Jane's mail and a few items Jane wanted from her condo. A story unspooled in her head as she drove.

There were once three princesses. Sisters. Held captive by an evil, or merely thoughtless, sorcerer. Each in a tower of ice separated from the others. They could but wave to one another over the glacial abyss that divided them. And their feet were always cold.

One day, by accident as she banged a pot on her balcony rail to shake loose day-old oatmeal, the middle sister began a drumming. The other sisters heard it and joined in, the three of them pounding a rhythm with their cooking pots.

Their drumming started a rumbling, and the rumbling became a shaking and the shaking became a swaying and the swaying became a tilting, until the three tall towers of ice toppled over, colliding into one another, filling the glacial abyss with shards and freeing the three princesses.

The princesses picked themselves up, fragments of ice shifting under their feet. Shy with each other at first, they refamiliarized themselves with their sisters' voices, noticing signs of age in one another's faces, then began talking over one another in sentences that began, "Do you remember?" Their voices, alike but different, echoed off the ice. And somewhere close by they heard a first trickle of water as sun warmed the long-frozen ground. A stream appeared, carving a blue path in the ice.

"Let us depart from this place," they said one to another. And hand in hand they set out, following the widening stream, until green grass appeared through thinning snow and they could shed their cloaks.

At Jane's place, a crow paced in the tree above the tenant mailboxes. Cora watched it pick its way along the branch, a tuxedoed man with his hands in his pockets. Its head bobbed as it strutted, and she wondered if all corvid heads bobbed like that, if she and Olin should tweak her raven's rings to make that movement.

She pulled Jane's mail from the box. The crow swooped down, dropping something at her feet, then flew off with a caw. It was an earring, the post bent. When she picked it up and rubbed away the dirt a small diamond glittered, reflecting in the metal of Olin's star.

Cora held it in her palm, expecting to feel a desire to pocket this thing that wasn't hers, but no urge came. She set it on top of the mailboxes for its owner to find.

She let herself into Jane's condo. The condo had a dish soap smell that Cora always associated with Jane. Not unpleasant, but not lovely either. Practical.

There was nothing urgent in today's mail. Cora set it on the counter. A large manila envelope caught her eye. Its return address was the lab that had done Walter's paternity test. Cora picked it up. It hadn't been opened. The red postmark was nearly a month old.

"You have got to be kidding me," she said out loud.

Cora drove to Bevins, where she found Rosie in the

dining room trying to tempt Walter to eat mac and cheese. Rosie looked up with a pleasant smile.

Cora slapped the envelope down on the table. "Look what our sister has had for a month."

"What is it?" Rosie scooped mac and cheese onto Walter's spoon, then laid it down and tapped the back of his hand to prompt him to eat. He picked it up and brought it to his mouth.

"The paternity test results. Can you believe her? Not telling us as soon as it arrived, and not telling us today? Here I was thinking what a great visit we had, how jolly Jane was for once. Turns out she was jolly because she was hiding this."

Rosie's mouth hung open. "What does it say?"

"I don't know yet. It's not opened."

"Well, open it!"

"I want to open it in front of Jane, see the expression on her face."

"How could she do that to us?" Rosie's voice rose. Walter watched her. He was thin, and seemed to have aged years since the last time Cora visited. He pulled the envelope toward him, and started to tear the corner.

Cora grabbed it away from him. "No, Dad!"

He folded his hands in his lap.

"I'm sorry," she said. "God, I wish he was with it enough to answer questions."

"Don't ask him anything or he might try to run off again," Rosie said, but Walter had grown so much more frail since his escape, the risk seemed low.

"It's okay, Dad, you don't need to worry." Rosie gave him another spoonful of mac and cheese. He got it to his mouth with trembling hands and chewed.

"Will you come with me back to Jane's?" Cora imagined the two of them confronting Jane. Would her sister feign ignorance? Offer excuses? Attack them for catching her? The possibilities fascinated Cora. She prepared for the show.

Rosie stood up. She kissed Walter on the head. "We have to go, Dad. Try to eat a little more, okay?"

As they left, Walter dipped his spoon in the mac and cheese for another bite.

Chapter 35

Walter was with Rosie the day of Rosie's grandmother's funeral, when Kiki showed up. Walter and Gary were in the yard waiting to drive Rosie to the church. Rosie's eyes were red from crying. Gary had his arm around her, whispering comfort into her hair. Walter wished he could console her, but he wasn't good at such things. The best he could do was transport her to the funeral.

Kiki came walking up the road with a dirty backpack slung over her shoulder, listing left and right, grabbing the fence to steady herself before she came up the drive. She was rail thin, her unwashed hair pulled off her face in a tight bun, the sleeves of her jean jacket rolled up to expose sores on her arms.

"Oh, shit," Gary said.

"You aren't supposed to be here, Kiki," Walter called as she approached. Rosie's grandmother Sandra had banned Kiki from the property years ago.

"I got every right to be here. My mama just died." Kiki's front teeth seemed to have crumbled in.

"Please don't ruin this day," Rosie said. "Not this one, please."

Kiki scratched her neck. "I come for her car. She promised it to me." Sandra's big Buick was parked under an old oak tree, where she'd left it the day she came home from shopping and told Rosie she was tired and going to lie down for a little bit. Kiki walked over to it and felt around inside the rear tire well. In triumph, she held up a small black magnetic box and fumbled the car's spare key out of it, dropping the two halves of the box on the ground. She opened the driver's side door.

"You're not taking that car, Kiki. It's Rosie's," Walter said.

"Watch me, dickhead. See y'all."

Walter started toward her but she was in the driver's seat with the door locked before he could reach her. He slapped the window. She gave him the finger and started the car.

She must have meant to reverse, but instead when she gunned it the car leapt forward, crashing into the trunk of the oak. The car alarm went off. Kiki tried to start it again but the engine wouldn't turn over. Sap bled from the oak's wounded bark and liquid of some kind leaked from under the Buick's hood. Cursing, Kiki opened the car door and got out. She lost her balance and sat down hard in the dirt, her head lolling back.

Walter jerked the key out of the ignition and silenced the car alarm. Now he could hear Rosie's hysterical crying. He rifled through Kiki's filthy backpack to try to see what she was on, finding two empty medication bottles and prescriptions from pill mills all up and down the East Coast.

Kiki struggled up and grabbed her backpack. "Give me that!" She staggered down the driveway and into the road.

Rosie hyperventilated. Gary held her tight.

"Take Rosie to the church," Walter instructed Gary. "I'm going to take care of this."

The Puppeteer's Daughters

He drove slowly up and down the wooded two-lane road until he spotted Kiki's jean jacket abandoned on the shoulder at the base of a bridge. He parked and scrambled down an embankment along a narrow path strewn with broken beer bottles and other trash.

He found Kiki passed out inside a cardboard refrigerator box under the bridge by a creek. It was clear she'd lived there a while. A pile of soiled clothes filled the corner. A stained towel draped the top of the box. The box smelled damp and sour. Bugs skittered. The only thing recognizable from Kiki's original life was the faded red thread tied around her wrist.

He shook her roughly to wake her up. She was even more fucked up than before, head rolling on her neck and eyes going to white. When she wouldn't wake up he took her arms and started to drag her out. She woke then, terrified. "Hey, stop it, man! You're hurting me! Police!"

He hauled her to his SUV and shoved her in the passenger seat. She struggled to focus. "Where we going?"

He didn't bother answering. There was a rehab place in Durham he'd seen advertised. It supported itself by running a moving company. It didn't require insurance or precertification. Kiki wouldn't be the first person dumped at its door.

Kiki passed out until he slowed down at the gates of the Lacy Street Rehabilitation Center. When she came to and saw where they were she started to fight. "No. I'm not going here." She grabbed for the door. He locked it from his side. A security guard waved them through. Kiki turned on Walter, hitting and scratching him. "Let me out, you bastard!"

He pulled up in front of the reception building, turned his engine off, then grabbed her by the throat and pushed her against the passenger seat. He held her there, her eyes bulging with fear, while he talked. "This was the last time. You will not show up at Rosie's again. You will not disrupt her life. You will never ruin another day for her. This is your home now." He hooked his finger under the rotten thread around her wrist and broke it, then let her go.

She snarled like a wild animal. "How do you know she's even yours?"

Staff from Lacy Street walked toward them. Walter got out and helped them extract Kiki from the passenger side. Two nurses led her away, still fighting. One of them asked her, "Ma'am, can you tell me what you took?"

Kiki turned back and screamed at Walter. "She's not even yours!"

He had missed the funeral. He went to the MacArthur Downs mansion, where he was staying like a guest in the suite farthest from Luciana's bedroom. He removed his suit jacket and brushed off the sand and stink from his struggle with Kiki.

Luciana reclined in the living room, reading a *Cosmopolitan* magazine. She barely paid attention when he told her what had happened.

"She had the nerve to imply Rosie wasn't mine," he finished.

Luciana looked up from her magazine. Now she was interested. "Is she?"

"Of course she is!" Kiki said it to hurt him, but Rosie looked like Walter's mother. The same dimples, the same lobeless ears.

"Because if she isn't, you don't owe her anything."

"That's not how it works," Walter said. You didn't turn your back on someone you had treated as your child, even if he hadn't always been the best father to Rosie.

Luciana went back to her magazine. "I'm simply saying, if you aren't her father, any obligation you might have to act like a father—say, to leave her anything—would be over and done."

Walter stared at Luciana, her polished nails, her synthetic-seeming blonde hair, the vapid copy that screamed from the pages of her magazine.

In fairy tales, fathers succumb to the whispered suggestions of their second wives, often at the expense of their children.

"I'm divorcing you," he said.

Chapter 36

At MacArthur Downs, Jane watched a video of her and Avril at age twelve playing putt-putt on the nine-hole course Walter had created by sinking tin cans around their yard at Ginkgo Street. Someone had given him a set of used clubs. She remembered the moldy smell of the canvas golf bag, the clatter when she and Avril dumped the clubs out on the ground, the little colored golf tees.

She heard the door open and Cora and Rosie walked in. Jane muted the video. "Back so soon? Did you get my stuff?"

"I got this." Cora held up a manila envelope.

"Oh," Jane said.

"What were you thinking?" Cora demanded. Beside her, Rosie glared at Jane with her arms crossed. Rosie had never glared at Jane like that before.

"Were you going to mention it?" Cora asked.

"I forgot about it," Jane said. It was true, in a way. She'd been so absorbed in watching Walter's home movies she hadn't thought about much else.

"Bullshit," Rosie said. Rosie never swore.

"We're going to open it now, and then we'll deal with you," Cora said.

It was a new, uncomfortable sensation for Jane to have her sisters gang up on her. She didn't like it.

Cora tore open the envelope and removed the pages inside. Rosie read over her shoulder.

"What does that mean, 'the alleged father is not excluded as the biological father of the tested child'?" Rosie asked.

"'Probability of paternity 99.9998 percent,'" Cora read. "It means he's the father. The XX means it's a female child."

"Let me see," Jane said, but Cora held the report out of her reach.

"So there's something to Dad's claim of a fourth daughter. It wasn't just the dementia inventing a child."

"Does the paper say who she is? Or who her mother is? Or her birth date?" Rosie said.

"Nothing like that," Cora said.

"See?" Jane said, relieved. "It doesn't matter that I didn't tell you right away. The report doesn't add anything to what we already knew. We aren't any closer to finding her than we were before."

"Shut up," Rosie snapped at her. "You should be ashamed of yourself."

"The test was done ten years ago," Cora said.

"So our sister is at least ten years old," Rosie said reverently. "God, I want to meet her so bad."

"What do we do next to find her?" Jane asked.

"There's no 'we.' You're off the case," Rosie said. "Me and Cora will find her."

"But I want to find her, too!" Jane said.

"Stop lying," Rosie said.

"Are you hiding anything else?" Cora asked.

"No!"

"You better not be. Rosie and I will decide next steps. Maybe a private investigator."

"What could a private investigator find that we couldn't?" Jane asked.

"A private investigator would have time to search," Cora said.

"And motivation," Rosie said. "He'd actually want to find her."

"If you're lucky we'll fill you in. Come on, Rosie," Cora said.

Cora and Rosie marched out. As they left, Jane heard Cora say, "That was fun." The door slammed.

Jane sat in the silence. She had never felt so lonely.

She struggled out of the recliner. She needed to do something to prove to her sisters that she wasn't against finding Walter's love child. She got her purse and the papers she needed and called an Uber to take her to the office of Walter's lawyer, Brenna Mabrey.

Jane knew Brenna from high school, and admired her. Brenna was a few years older, tall and graceful, a girl who studied on Friday nights while Jane and Avril drank beer, who disdained cliques and drama.

Walter was Brenna's very first client when she joined her father's firm after law school. Walter was friends with her late father, Bruce, and when Sharper Image offered Walter a merchandising deal after his third *The Tonight Show* appearance, Bruce assigned the contract review to Brenna. Gray Steed had since retained a cadre of Manhattan intellectual property and entertainment lawyers, but Brenna still handled Walter's personal affairs.

Jane hobbled in on her crutches. Brenna's hair had turned snow white in her twenties except for a wide black streak in her bangs. Back then, people called the gray premature. Now it was age-appropriate. She had gained weight, but there was still an elegance to the way her long bones moved through space when she greeted Jane.

"I was just thinking about you," Brenna said. "My husband and I saw Brett play with the Addled Pigs the other night. He was great!"

"He's dropped out of school with one semester to go. I could wring his neck," Jane said.

"Ouch. Well, he's young enough that there aren't many mistakes he can't recover from. And it may not be a mistake, Jane. He's really talented." Brenna gestured around her office, which displayed the framed album covers, paintings, and novels of the artists she represented. "Success happens when talent meets opportunity. And luck, of course. He might just make it."

Jane respected Brenna too much to yell *Shut up!*

"Anyway, what can I help you with?" Brenna asked.

Jane showed Brenna Walter's codicil, with his angry cursive imposing conditions on her and her sisters.

Brenna touched her forehead. "I didn't know about this."

"Is it valid?" Jane asked.

"Unfortunately, yes. North Carolina honors holographic—handwritten—wills. If he'd showed it to me I would have advised him to tear it up. I'm sorry."

"There's something else I need to ask you about. At his birthday party, he alluded to a fourth daughter, and we found a positive paternity test in his things." Jane left out the part about hiding the paternity test from her sisters.

"He never mentioned another child to me," Brenna said, but Jane could sense there was something she wasn't telling.

"What is it?"

Brenna twisted her mouth to the side. "There were a couple of times, years ago, when he insisted on seeing my dad instead of me. I assumed it was something medical that he was embarrassed to share with a woman. Wait here and let me see if I can find anything in my dad's old files."

While Brenna was gone Jane looked around the office. On Brenna's desk was a carved puppet head that Jane recognized as one of Walter's. Jane couldn't help it; she picked it up. The round, smooth wood felt good in her hands. A woman's features, lips parted in the half-smile characteristic of Walter's female marionettes, prominent, intricate ears.

He had stopped carving after Zeno made him famous, putting his marionettes out of his mind the way some men do when they leave a first family for a second, the walling-off the only way to live with the deep guilt of the abandonment. This must have been one he never finished.

Brenna returned, carrying a dusty file. She smiled at Jane holding the puppet head. "It's one of my favorites. When I'm stressed I hold it like you're doing now."

Jane set the head back on the desk.

Brenna sat down and opened the file. "Dad wasn't the most organized, but I found this." She hesitated. "It's privileged."

"I'm his power of attorney. I waive the privilege."

Brenna nodded. "Apparently, he didn't want you girls to know. He set up an endowment at the Lacy Street Rehab

Center, basically a trust for Kiki, to assure her a place to live until she died if she needed it. They can't kick her out."

"Any other trusts?" Jane asked, thinking she would follow the money to her lost sister.

"Not through our firm, as far as I can tell," Brenna said. "You could check the accounting department at Gray Steed. He might have arranged to pay some things through the company."

Jane doubted Cora would know, but Alice might. She felt a sudden, strong longing to find their sister. "What would you do if you were us and looking for a lost relative?"

"Good question." Brenna crooked a finger over her mouth as she thought. "There is this one guy we've used a few times to locate heirs and missing deadbeat dads."

"Great," Jane said. "What's the name?"

"Wilkie Bozer," Brenna told her. "Fair warning, he's odd. Very odd. And if he smells money he'll try to upcharge you. But every time I've used him he's found the person." She scribbled a phone number and handed it to Jane. She set the puppet head on Walter's file as a paperweight.

Jane waved a hand at the artwork on the walls, the shelved books of Brenna's clients. "Do you do any art yourself?"

Brenna shook her head. "No time. And no talent."

"Practicing law must be an art, though," Jane offered.

"Not really. Lawyers solve problems. We see the world in terms of what needs to be fixed and we fix it. We're useful, but we don't create anything. That's why I like representing people like your dad. It allows me to hover near the makers."

Jane looked at the puppet head again and realized it wasn't a generic piece that Walter had decided not to use. The carving was a young Brenna.

The Puppeteer's Daughters

Brenna smiled at Jane, her tired eyes bright and watchful. "Tell Brett to call me if anybody offers him a recording contract."

❧

PETE PHONED WHILE JANE WAITED FOR AN UBER TO TAKE HER back to the MacArthur Downs mansion. "Where are you? I went by the house and you weren't there. I was worried."

"I had to see Dad's lawyer. I'm headed back now. But I'm not going to stay. I'm sick of that place. I want to go home."

"Can you manage the stairs?"

"I'll figure it out."

"I'll wait here for you. Help you pack up. I can drive you to your condo whenever you're ready."

In college, Jane had dated Pete's roommate before she dated Pete. Cy was a man of many causes, always doing good. He woke early on Saturdays to collect expired food from grocery stores for the homeless. He marched against apartheid. He registered students to vote. He was late—hours late—to every date they ever scheduled and Jane didn't feel she could complain because who was she to demand he spend time with her at the expense of orphans and widows? If she wanted time with him she had to tag along to his protests and errands of mercy.

One Saturday when Jane, Cy, and Pete were supposed to take a chartered bus to a women's rights march in Washington, DC, Jane woke up with a wretched cold. Cy patted her on the head, careful not to get too close, and he and Pete left for the march. Half an hour later, Pete knocked on Jane's dorm room door with a quart of hot matzo ball soup.

Jane held a wad of tissues to her nose. "What are you doing here?"

"You were sick," Pete said. "Try this, it'll make you feel better."

"You skipped the march to bring me soup?"

"You were sick," Pete repeated.

In the years they spent together after that day, Pete never put anything ahead of Jane. Not a cause, not work ambitions, not even music or pot. He would abandon any of those things in a second if Jane or their boys needed him. She had forgotten that.

When the Uber let Jane off at the MacArthur Downs house, Pete was standing in the driveway.

"Don't you have better things to do than wait on me?" she asked.

"No," he said. "No."

He helped her pack and they drove to her condo.

"Did you see the link Brett sent?" Pete asked. "The Addled Pigs are performing one of his songs."

"I didn't open it," Jane said.

"You should. It's awesome."

"Which song?" Jane asked.

"A new one. 'Equations for a Happy Life.'"

Pete pulled up in front of her condo. "Can you really handle those stairs?"

"I'm happy to be home. I'll be careful."

"Anything you need, I can bring you. I could even, you know, stay with you for a few days."

She frowned.

He sighed. "I've been thinking, a lot. About you and

me. It's like, there's no good reason why we're not still together."

"You gave me reasons, Pete."

"I know, I know. I did dumb stuff. But I'm not doing dumb stuff now. I miss you."

"We're divorced. That was hard but we did it. I don't want to undo it. There's a lot of things I like about being single. This condo, for one. Not having to share my money." *Not getting hurt or surprised again when you do something stupid and don't tell me.*

"We don't have to be married. Or even live together. I could just be your boyfriend." He put his hand over hers. "Think about it." He got out of the car and retrieved her crutches from the back seat.

Jane flexed her fingers. It had been a long time since anyone held her hand.

After Pete helped her struggle up the stairs and left, Jane sat in her living room with her throbbing foot elevated. Outside, she could hear two neighbors flirting, their laughter cut off by the closing of a door. She pulled out her cell phone and found the video Brett had emailed.

Brett's sinewy arms held the guitar as if he had happened upon it and picked it up out of curiosity. He played with calm concentration. The music was beautiful, even on a tinny cell phone.

Jane rested her ear on her phone to listen.

Chapter 37

Rosie invited Cora back to her house so Cora wouldn't have to hang out with Jane at MacArthur Downs. Rosie liked this new alliance. As they pulled in, Gary dropped Madison off. He waved but didn't stop to say hello. Madison ran to hug Cora, then Rosie. She smelled like vanilla ice cream. They went in the house and Rosie sent Madison to wash her hands.

"Wow," Cora said, looking around the kitchen at the college brochures that drooped from the ceiling and the pennants that plastered the refrigerator. Madison's graduation gown was spread over a chair waiting for Rosie to hem it. "What is all this?"

"It's my inspiration," Rosie said. "I focus on Madison's future and it keeps me from overeating."

"It's working," Cora said, sitting down. "I can tell you've lost weight. Your face is thinner."

It was the first time anybody had commented, and it made Rosie feel good. "Thank you. I'm getting used to not popping everything in my mouth."

Madison came back. She stood next to Rosie's chair, dancing from one leg to the other.

"What you need, baby?" Rosie asked her.

"I have a secret," Madison said.

"What is it?"

"Daddy said not to tell." Madison looked about to pop.

Rosie put an arm out and brought Madison in for a hug.

"We don't keep secrets. Daddy shouldn't have asked you to. Go on and tell me."

Madison hopped on her tiptoes. "I'm going to have a little brother!"

Rosie's throat filled. It was difficult to breathe. Everything in the room seemed to waver as if she were standing in a road on a hot day. She was burning up.

Cora's eyes were even with hers. "When?" Cora asked Madison.

"Next month!" Madison said.

Cora took Rosie's hand but Rosie hardly felt it. "That soon?" Cora said. "That's exciting for you. Madison, honey, can you go outside and pick us some flowers?" Madison danced outside.

Rosie struggled up from her chair and went to the fridge. It's handle felt sticky in her hand. When she ripped off the layers of pennants and tape, the cold air soothed her face. She took out a tub of Cool Whip and peeled back the lid, got a spoon from the drain board and sat down at the table. She stabbed the spoon into the topping.

Cora pulled her chair around next to Rosie. She put both of her hands over Rosie's to keep them where they were.

Chapter 38

Cora answered Jane's call. "This is not a good time." She could hear Rosie sobbing in the bathroom.

"I know you're mad at me, but I have news," Jane said.

"It's not a good time." Cora stepped out on the porch where Rosie couldn't overhear. "Gary knocked up his girlfriend. The baby's due next month. Rosie's pretty torn up."

"Shit," Jane said.

"What's your news?"

"Brenna Mabrey gave me the name of an investigator. We can get in to see him tomorrow."

Rosie came outside, wiping her eyes with a towel, her face blotchy and mottled.

"I don't think that will work. Rosie won't feel up to it," Cora said.

"Who is it?" Rosie asked. Cora told her.

"It's fine. I'll go," Rosie said.

"Are you sure?" Cora asked, concerned for Rosie.

"I want to find her," Rosie blubbered. "She's family."

"Okay," Cora said to Jane. "We'll meet you there. Text me the address and time. I won't be back at MacArthur Downs tonight."

"Don't stay away on my account," Jane said. "I'm back at my condo."

Cora watched Rosie lower herself to the porch steps and take deep, forced breaths, trying to control her crying. Cora sat down beside her. She put her arm around Rosie's shoulders. "I'm going to stay with Rosie anyway. She shouldn't be alone tonight."

🐟

STANDING WITH JANE AND ROSIE ON THE FIVE HUNDRED BLOCK of South Wilmington Street the next afternoon, Cora wondered what passersby must make of them: three such different-looking women staring at the facades of the appliance store and the boarded-up dry cleaners, and then at the slip of paper Jane held, and then back at the baffling store fronts. A stranger wouldn't peg them for sisters and wouldn't pause long enough to see them turn the handle of a shabby door wedged between the two businesses and go inside.

They climbed the stairs to the second floor where, on a narrow landing, a frosted glass door bore the lettering: WILKIE BOZER, FORENSIC GENEALOGIST. Jane knocked and upon hearing a muffled "Come in!" they entered.

The office was something out of another time. Unicorns and maidens danced on rich red carpet in need of vacuuming. A desk and matching credenza crouched on carved claw-and-ball legs. A black fur hat gathered dust on an antlered coat rack. Old books covered every surface, many of them open and displaying ancient spidery handwriting, and yet as the occupant of the office swiveled toward them and closed his desk drawer, Cora heard the unmistakable chime of an Apple device.

The man appeared to be in his early seventies, plump, his shoulders rounded with kyphosis under a moss-green cardigan. He had rather a lot of hair growing in his ears. Cora wanted to tell him there were products for that, spa treatments.

"You must be the Gray sisters. Do sit down. Wilkie Bozer at your service." He had an extreme Southern accent, the kind heard only in cartoons, that he had either acquired by aristocratic birth in low country South Carolina or made up. He pulled an old chest around to make a third visitor's chair. "Do excuse the makeshift seating. I rarely have three clients at one time. People tend to seek out my services . . . privately."

Cora perched on the trunk while Jane and Rosie took the chairs.

"So." He put his hands together. The nail on his right pointer finger looked recently gnawed. "What can I do for you?"

"We're looking for a family member." Jane explained what they knew, and what they didn't.

"Fascinating. And your father isn't able to tell you anything more?"

"No," Rosie said.

"Where has your father spent his time? In what cities might he have had . . . relations?"

"Here. New York. And he used to travel widely. Paris, London, Moscow, the Czech Republic. Once to China."

"Our father is Walter Gray," Cora said.

Mr. Bozer raised his eyebrows, causing his hairy ears to lift. "Oh! *That* Gray." His pupils glittered. "When the client is a celebrity, confidentiality and discretion are paramount. There will be a small additional fee . . ."

"We'll pay the same fee you would charge anyone else," Jane said.

Mr. Bozer coughed, chastened. "Very well. I prefer to search paper records. I've had my best success that way, but in a case like yours when we know nothing about the missing relative, DNA testing is your best option." He reached in his desk drawer and pulled out kits with the Gene23 logo on them. "This company has the largest database. You daughters and your father each provide saliva samples. We send them off—I can get them expedited. Then I follow up with any positive hits we get from people whose specimens share your father's DNA."

"But they have to have taken the same test, right?" Cora asked.

"Yes."

"So if our sister is just a little kid, it could be years," Rosie said. "Or never."

"Correct," Mr. Bozer said. "But you might get lucky. If you do, there are additional considerations."

"Like what?" Jane asked.

Mr. Bozer sighed. "Sometimes these searches can expose . . . divergent interests."

They waited for him to explain.

"You have to be prepared for the results. There are surprises more often than you'd think. Heirs find themselves unentitled, genetically set adrift. Usurpers are legitimized. Sisters discover they are not sisters."

Rosie started to cry.

Mr. Bozer used the snaggled nail of his pointer finger to turn the page of an ancient ledger that lay open on the desk in front of him. Brittle paper flaked in his hand and he crushed it into a puff of dust. The frosted pane of the door rattled and a thread of cold air snaked along the back of Cora's neck. She shivered. Mr. Bozer seemed to be looking directly at her. Jane and Rosie sat motionless, as if captured in time.

"Shall I find her for you at any cost, Miss Gray?" His Southern accent had disappeared.

The molecules in the room between Cora and Mr. Bozer seemed to enlarge like oily pores. Images flickered through her mind. Walter's laugh behind the camera as Jane and Rosie performed *Amahl*. Him shouting at Cora not to let the marionettes hug. Olin ducking his head to miss the door frame as he left the Gray Steed archive room the last time they spoke. A single tear suspended now on Rosie's cheek.

"No," Cora said. She would pay a high cost, but not any cost. Beside her, Jane and Rosie stirred. Rosie wiped her eyes.

"I don't think we'll use your services after all," Jane said, looking at her sisters. "Will we?"

Cora and Rosie nodded their agreement.

"We'll pay you for the kits." Cora swept them into her lap and counted cash from her wallet.

"Suit yourself," Mr. Bozer said, his disarming Southern accent returning as she handed him the money. "Just be clear in your own minds what you want out of this."

Back outside on the sidewalk, Jane said, "What a creep."

Cora distributed the DNA kits. "We'll search for her ourselves, even if it takes years."

"I can get Dad's sample," Jane offered.

"No. I'll do it. Give me your specimens now and I'll send all of them in at once." Cora could tell she'd hurt Jane's feelings but she didn't trust Jane.

While Jane and Rosie spit in the plastic vials, Cora checked her phone, hoping for a text from Olin. Nothing. She started to text him but wasn't sure what to say.

🐦

AT BEVINS, CORA REMOVED HER SUITCASE FROM THE TRUNK OF the SUV. She had packed her servant puppet along with two others, with thoughts of practicing the new mechanism while she was in Raleigh, and perhaps entertaining her father. She hadn't risked bringing the raven puppet. It was too precious. Post 9/11, air travel was precarious for puppeteers. Using superglue on a piece would set off the chemical alarms. The weird shapes on the X-ray machine alarmed TSA workers, who were clumsy and doltish in rifling through a puppeteer's stuff.

She'd placed the servant puppet's metal mechanism in a plastic Ziplock bag with a note telling the TSA what it was, and folded the puppet's body in cloth so they'd know how to repack it. She'd prayed her luggage would make it to Raleigh when she did. Many a puppeteer had arrived in a city for a show and learned that their star puppet hadn't made it. She knew puppeteers who refused to fly at all. When she landed at the Raleigh-Durham airport she unzipped her suitcase right there on the floor at baggage claim to make sure her puppets had survived the journey. They had.

The Puppeteer's Daughters

Walter sat at a table in the dining room with an elderly woman who slumped half-asleep in a wheelchair. He systematically tore his paper placemat into long strips. Staff was busy preparing lunch in the connected kitchen. A thick smell of institutional food hung in the air.

An aide with a lovely Caribbean accent set a cup of Ensure in front of Walter and hugged his shoulders. "Now you drink this, Mr. Gray. Make me proud."

Walter smiled. He clearly liked this kind aide. He knew the CNAs more than his daughters, because they cleaned and comforted him every day.

Cora approached the table, rolling her suitcase. Walter looked up. He seemed to know Cora, though she would never assume he could remember her name. "It's Cora, Dad," she said, kissing him on the cheek and sitting down. "I've come for a visit."

"Isn't that nice, Mr. Gray?" the aide said. "You are the younger daughter?"

"Yes, I'm Cora. I live in New York."

"I am Fabiola. We love your father. What a legacy he has built for you and your sisters."

Cora thought about what her father had transmitted to her. The wealth and reputation of Gray Steed Puppets, of course, but also an innate instinct to look for the new in the old, to transform one thing into another or invent something unique from air. By selling Gray Steed to pursue her own art, would she be destroying his legacy or continuing it? And what would Jane and Rosie name as his legacy to them?

Fabiola left to help another resident. Cora took the DNA kit from her purse. "Dad, can you do something for me?

Work up your spit like this." She swished her own saliva around in her mouth and he imitated her. "Now spit it in this cup." He obeyed, looking over the cup rim at her.

She screwed the lid on his sample. "Thanks."

"Welcome," he said.

Cora took her puppets out of her suitcase and assembled them. Walter's eyes widened in delight. The little woman who shared his table perked up and leaned forward to look.

Cora slipped the servant puppet on her hand and made him bow and look around. "What do you think?"

Walter laughed. At least Cora thought it was a laugh, a breathless cackle, his eyes damp with tears or old age; she couldn't tell.

He reached greedily for the puppet. "Is this? Is this?"

Cora helped him fit the rings on his fingers. He had tremors in his hands now, a puppeteer's nightmare. If she gave him a marionette control, the marionette would flail with dystonia, but Cora's puppet, somewhat too small for him, contained his trembling. No one could operate the puppet like Cora, but Walter fiddled with the rings, creating some interesting expressive gestures. "Look at this what-not!" he cried.

"Dad." Cora whispered so no one nearby could hear. "Disney offered to buy Gray Steed."

Walter tugged the rings to make the puppet throw its arms wide.

"What should I do?" She longed for his guidance, his blessing.

He held the puppet high, turning it this way and that. The old woman who shared his table pointed to it, talking, but

The Puppeteer's Daughters

Parkinson's had quieted her voice so that Cora couldn't hear what she said. Bevins was a place where words were lost: her father's to dementia, the old woman's to the air that refused to carry her speech to the small bones of a listener's ear.

Cora gently disentangled Walter's fingers from the rings. She slipped the puppet on her right hand and put a fur hat on its head. She would operate her female puppet, a woman in a Victorian dress, with her left. She lay a third puppet, a boy, on the table to trade out when the story called for him. She worked the puppets so that Walter and the old woman could both see.

"There was once a Sound Seeker," she said. She had to swallow around the lump in her throat to continue.

There was once a Sound Seeker who could find lost sounds: the burble of a long-dry spring, the trill of spring peepers to cheer a winter's day, the splash of a stone skipped six times on childhood water. If he walked, and was quiet, the sounds would come to him like birds, sometimes in minutes, sometimes in days. Once, it took a year to find a boy's sweet soprano, lost after his voice changed. When the Sound Seeker found it, the voice was tired and hungry but excited with stories to tell. The client, the boy's mother, wept with happiness.

The Sound Seeker could find any sound, but words—lost, misheard, or forgotten—were his mainstay. Promises mouthed across a crowded train platform as the train blew its whistle, endearments murmured at waking when the ears weren't primed to understand, wisdom spoken in a visitation dream then lost when the sleeper rolled over on the pillow. "It's the change of position," he cautioned. "The slosh of cranial fluids washes the dream away. Lie still and remember before you move."

His clients sought lyrics to songs, that one ingredient for a secret family recipe, directions to treasure they had buried, but mostly these words: "I love you."

"Those three little syllables seem to get misplaced more than any others," he would say. "They are quite my bread and butter."

It was those three words that led a woman to the Sound Seeker's shop on a sultry summer afternoon. The heat had caused her to remember a night long ago, when she and her lover made love in the park across from her mother's house, she on his lap, her striped dress pulled up above her thighs, streetlamps illuminating the park's fountain but allowing her and her friend the cover of shadow.

Walking back, her lover took her hands and danced her along the middle of the road. He said something to her in Spanish, a language he knew from his travels. She didn't catch it and asked him to repeat it but he wouldn't. If he had, she might have understood. She knew the word amor *and could have listened for it on second repetition. But he wouldn't speak, perhaps already regretting the utterance, if what he said was in fact "I love you."*

She had forgotten that night, and that lover, but as today's humidity tugged her hair into curls, she felt a fierce yearning for both.

The bell over the door tinkled when she entered the Sound Seeker's shop. He was speaking to another customer, a bereft young man. "I cannot help you if your father never spoke the words." The young man ducked past the woman and out the door, in tears.

The woman told the Sound Seeker what she wanted.

"Since the words were spoken in another tongue, I will have to unbend them when I find them, in order for you to understand," he said. "There will be a small additional fee."

The Puppeteer's Daughters

She readily agreed, and the Sound Seeker set off in search of her lover's words. He found them easily, in a tree near the park where they were first spoken. He coaxed them down and sent a message to the woman to come for them.

When she arrived at the shop, the Sound Seeker was holding her lover's words. "Are you sure you want to hear them?" he asked. "I cannot be responsible if he was asking you to pass the milk."

The woman held still for a moment, considering her choice.

When her lover left that night for a three-month voyage, she was important to him. When he returned, she wasn't. She met his ship thinking she would have him to herself. The smell of tropical travel was strong on his body. He had her drive the carriage to a homecoming party for his traveling companions. At the party was the ship captain's young daughter, whom he had comforted on their travels when a local man overstepped his bounds and frightened her. The woman's lover had saved the girl and she worshiped him. He liked being worshiped.

The woman's lover had spoken his words to her in summer and they had dissipated on a humid breeze. If he had uttered them in winter, maybe they would have frozen in the air long enough for her to hear him say he loved her.

She nodded to the Sound Seeker and he began to untwist the sound, gently so its strands wouldn't break with their bending back.

The woman leaned close, cupping her ears. This time, she would not miss the words.

Cora lowered the puppets to her lap. Walter clapped his hands. "Brah . . . brah . . ."

"Bravo," Cora prompted him.

"Bravo!" he echoed.

The old woman stared at the now-silent puppets, rapt. Her lips moved in an "Oh!"

Cora leaned close and could just make out her words. "Beautiful, beautiful!"

Chapter 39

Jane called Avril. "I need a favor. Tell me when the neighbor at my house is gone."

"What are we going to do?" Avril asked, instantly on board. Jane told her about the putt-putt video. "I want to see if the cans are still there."

"Oh my God, the putt-putt course. That was so fun. I'll start spying right now."

Avril called the next day. "The neighbor left. Want to come over?"

"Yes!"

Jane took an Uber to Ginkgo Street, guiding the driver the back way past the split-levels and modest brick ranches that had been affordable to families with kids and stay-at-home moms. It had been a great neighborhood for bicycles. Flat and safe. Jane and Avril had biked everywhere growing up, to school and Lake Johnson and Keith's Grocery to buy candy. Their calves were rock hard.

The Uber pulled up to the curb and Jane struggled out with her crutches. Avril waved from the porch of the house she'd bought from her parents when they moved to Florida. "Lemme get my trowel!" She disappeared inside.

Jane hobbled to where she could see the backyard of her old house. The new owner had razed Ernestine's tangled garden patch and manicured the lawn.

Whenever Jane and Avril reminisced about their

childhood, Avril brought up the pine needle tea. At the height of the Euell Gibbons Grape-Nuts years, Walter and Ernestine had owned all of Gibbons' books and ate various things that grew in their yard. On a Saturday morning when Avril slept over, Walter sent Jane and Avril outside to pick pine needles he could make into tea. Avril thought it was the coolest thing ever. Jane was mortified. She wanted to switch houses with Avril, whose mom packed her lunch with tiny bags of Fritos, Snack Pack puddings, and individually packaged Hostess Ho Hos, with a paraffin chocolate skin that Avril peeled off and ate first before the cake.

They picked needles from the tree, sap sticky on their hands, and brought them to Walter, who boiled them in a pot on the stove. He wore sweatpants and a threadbare T-shirt that said "Property of NCSU Gym." He hadn't showered or shaved and there was more gray in his whiskers than on his head. He made them pancakes out of soybean flour he'd ground himself from beans that spilled from a fifty-pound bag in the pantry. When the tea was ready he served it in mismatched china teacups.

"This is delicious, Mr. Gray!" Avril said.

Walter transformed his spatula into a puppet with a high British voice like Queen Elizabeth. "Why thank you, my dear!"

"Stop being stupid," Jane heard herself say.

"How dare you!" the Queen spatula huffed indignantly, making Avril laugh. Walter was showing off for Avril, approximating his idea of a good dad. Jane sipped her resin-flavored water, anxious that Walter couldn't pull it off. She met his eyes above the puppet, and saw in them exasperation at her but also resignation that she might be right, that he was bound to slip up.

He laid the spatula to rest in the sink.

Balancing on her crutches now, Jane did the math: when her father made the pine needle tea, he was younger than she was now. The calculation allowed her to feel a compassion for Walter that she hadn't felt when she was thirteen. Then, he was a grown-up and was supposed to know how to behave. Now, she could see him as a person, a parent, and she wished she had been less hard on him.

Avril jogged across the road, carrying a trowel. "What are we, twelve?" she said, giggling.

Jane couldn't squat with her boot and crutches so she stood guard while Avril dug. Finding the holes proved harder than they expected. There was no sign of any of the nine holes on the surface and they disagreed about where Walter had sunk the cans.

"I swear there was one near the spigot. Let me dig around." Avril crouched down.

Jane poked a crutch in the dirt. "What will your neighbor think when she finds holes in her yard?"

"Moles," Avril said, scraping with her trowel. "Wait, I hit something." She dug out a clump of earth, barely recognizable as a rusted can completely full of compressed dirt. She washed it off under the neighbor's spigot and held it up to Jane. There was hardly any metal left. The rims remained, connected by a filigree of brown rust. Jane took it from Avril like a precious treasure and held it dripping up to the light. She could see through it like lace.

A car door slammed behind her. Avril froze. "Shit."

Jane turned around. Avril's neighbor walked up the driveway, carrying a Michael's bag with skeins of yarn peeping out. She looked puzzled.

Avril stood up and waved. "Hi Francine!"

Francine approached cautiously. "What's going on?"

"You remember Jane?" Avril asked.

"Oh. Sure. How's your father?" Francine said.

"He's fine, thank you. Hasn't run away again." Jane smiled.

Francine squinted at Avril's muddy hands, the rivulet of brown water running under her spigot. "Is there some problem?"

Avril babbled an explanation about searching for the long-lost putt-putt course. "You know, Jane's father is Walter Gray."

"Who?"

"Walter Gray. The famous puppeteer?"

"Oh," Francine said. "I always thought puppets were kinda creepy."

Avril muttered into her hand. "Oh no she didn't."

Of all the phrases Jane's father hated most, "puppets are creepy" was the most incendiary.

"You don't know shit about puppetry," Jane said.

Francine's eyes widened.

Jane pointed to the yarn in the woman's shopping bag. "You knit? Good for you. My father designed, engineered, sewed, carved, welded, wrote, sang, directed, acted, filmed, and innovated. He helped bring American puppetry to the world stage. He made his first national TV appearance while we lived in this house. Instead of calling puppets 'creepy' you should put up a damn plaque."

"Preach it!" Avril said.

"Could you get off my property now?" Francine asked, her voice wobbly.

"I'm taking *this*," Jane said, holding up the rusted can.

Francine looked as if she was about to cry. "Please don't come back for the rest of them."

Avril carried the can so Jane could operate her crutches.

"Way to go to bat for Walter," Avril said. "I know you have issues with how your dad treated you versus Cora, but you have to admit, a putt-putt course in your yard is pretty cool. At some point, we all have to appreciate what our parents did give us and stop resenting what they couldn't."

"Oh, shut up," Jane said.

Chapter 40

With Cora back in New York and Jane still not able to drive, Rosie took it on herself to check on Walter and try to coax him to eat. Her motive was mixed. She hated to see him failing, and she could hear the clock ticking. She was the only daughter whose inheritance was time-sensitive. Jane could draw eyes on her fist with a pen and make a puppet as Walter breathed his last. Cora's directive to "live among the humans" was too vague to hold her to. But Rosie's condition was measurable. At the rate she was losing weight, Walter would need to live to a hundred. And from what the director of nursing said, that wasn't likely. Rosie didn't want to be one of those people who thought about money when she should care about her father's health. But it wasn't just the money. It was her chance to become a legitimate member of the family. That's what was ticking away.

She poured her homemade gravy over Wonder Bread and cut it into bite-size pieces, spoon-feeding Walter the first bite so he'd know what he was missing. He smacked his lips and took the spoon from her for the next bite.

Too bad you couldn't donate fat like you could organs. That would solve both their problems. Walter would have the stores he needed, and Rosie would be skinny. Like Amber.

Rosie couldn't help comparing herself to Amber. Amber wasn't any nicer or sexier or richer than Rosie. She had exactly one thing Rosie didn't—she was thin. No, she had another thing Rosie lacked. She had Gary. And Rosie didn't even get a full nine months to prepare herself for this new baby. Amber was one of those scrawny women who didn't show. Gary had hidden the pregnancy from Rosie all these months even when he was coming over for sex. Rosie teared up. She really had to get a grip on herself. She wiped her eyes with the back of her hand.

"Rosie, are you okay?" Jane stood there with her crutches. She must not have trusted Rosie to look after Walter in her absence.

"I'm fine," Rosie said, but she wasn't. Her eyes stung and her nose ran.

Jane sat down. She touched Walter's arm. "Hey Dad, it's me. Jane."

Walter gave a little smile but focused on the gravy.

"I hope he hasn't forgotten who I am," Jane said. "Seriously, are you okay?"

"I don't know. Maybe I'm just hungry. This durn diet. Look at that pretty gravy and I'm not supposed to eat any of it, but I probably will, and then I'll gain back any weight I've lost this week and I'll never lose what I'm supposed to and I won't get anything in the will that I can use for Madison, and I'll always be *fat*." Rosie blew her nose into a napkin.

"He shouldn't have put that in the will."

"But he did," Rosie said.

"Look how he's eating." Jane pointed. Walter had finished the bread and lifted his plate to lick it. "Thank you so much, Rosie. Your gravy is a much better calorie-delivery system than Ensure."

"Thanks," Rosie said. "Anyway. I have something for you." Rosie fished in her bag and gave one graduation invitation to Jane and another to Walter. She was a Jostens preferred customer by now and had gotten twenty percent off the formal invitations. She'd already invited Cora, Gary's brother, and Ernestine—not Gary and Amber. They could throw their own party. She'd sent one to Nelson from the weight loss center, because she liked him and if he was around she wouldn't be tempted to eat too much at the party. She wished she could invite their missing sister.

"The graduation is at Madison's kindergarten, then I figured we'd do the party here at Bevins so Dad can see everybody," she said.

"Nice. I'll be there," Jane said.

Walter turned his invitation this way and that, trying to figure it out. Then he ripped it in two without opening it.

"Figures," Rosie said, tearing up again.

Jane took the invitation away from Walter. "Don't read anything into it. It's just what he does. Look Dad, Madison is graduating." Jane showed him the torn card.

"It doesn't matter," Rosie said.

Walter blinked at Rosie with watery eyes. He reached for the gravy jar. Rosie poured more on his plate.

"We'll get around his will. There has to be a way," Jane said.

Chapter 41

The night Luciana leapt at the suggestion that Rosie wasn't his, Walter left the house in his SUV, which still smelled of Kiki's sweat. Luciana didn't understand that Rosie had saved him. She had come along just as Jane was leaving him, entering those preteen years when she shut him out and formed an alliance with Ernestine that didn't include him, behind a barricade of feminine hygiene products and lowered toilet lids. Even before puberty, Jane had been a secret-keeper, guarding parts of herself, disapproving of him. Since she was a toddler she had worn a scowl that creased her brow. Now that vertical furrow was deep and permanent.

As Jane rebuffed him, he came to treasure Rosie. She was open and loving where Jane was aloof, laughed spontaneously while Jane was more inclined to snort. When Rosie sat on his lap or stood close to him to show him a flower or bug she had found, she calmed him. She accepted him in a way Jane didn't, maybe because Rosie's expectations of him had never been high. He hadn't disappointed her like he had Jane.

Of course Rosie grew up as well, leaving him for Gary. Even Cora separated from him in turn, though she was following in his footsteps. He acknowledged he had been a better father to all three girls when they were small, before they developed minds of their own. It was the marionettist in him, wanting to control their movements and thoughts.

He distinctly remembered how it had surprised him the first time Jane refused to do as he ordered. He had taken her to the park to ride her bike. When it was time to go he said something that made her mad and she turned into a demon, screaming at him and marching off into the neighborhood above the park. He didn't know what to do. He couldn't drag her back by force without someone calling the cops or social services. He hung out by the van for two hours, getting dirty looks from suspicious park moms, until Jane finally appeared up the street, came to the van, and got in the passenger seat, slamming the door. She didn't speak to him on the ride home. That was the last time he took her to the park. He took Rosie instead. At least he thought he had. He couldn't specifically remember pushing Rosie on the swings or waiting for her at the bottom of the slide, but he hoped he had. If he didn't, he should have.

He drove to the home of his friend, lawyer Bruce Mabrey, and asked Bruce how to legitimize Rosie. Up until then he had thought Luciana tolerated Rosie, even though she didn't welcome her. Now he realized Rosie was in danger, from Luciana and maybe even Ernestine. If he didn't do something, the stepmothers might try to disinherit Rosie after he died, banish her to the hearth to rake cinders while their own daughters thrived. He wouldn't allow it, and he wouldn't allow Kiki to claim he wasn't Rosie's father.

Bruce told Walter how to get a DNA test and arranged to file Walter's acknowledgment of paternity with the court. Walter couldn't ask Rosie for a cheek swab, but he had a water bottle she'd left in his car. He took that to the lab and paid for an expedited test. When it came back a match, as he knew it would, he went and found Luciana, who had claimed the downstairs while they waited for their attorneys to duke out who would get the MacArthur Downs house.

He flapped the paternity test in Luciana's face. "Rosie *is* mine, and I've made it official."

Luciana grabbed at the paternity test, ripping it. "You think I care, you stupid old man? Enjoy your final years with no one but your fat daughter to keep you company."

Walter almost slapped her, his hand coming alive on its own like Punch wielding a club. She flinched and he stopped himself.

"Don't mess with my girls," he said. "Any of them."

Chapter 42

A lice stirred two gin and tonics and set one down near Cora. "Have you made any decisions about the Disney offer?"

Cora laid out her puppets. "I'm close."

"Did your dad have anything to say?"

"He doesn't say much these days."

Alice settled in her chair. "What do you have for me?" There was no sunset to see today. Only darkening gray sky and rain spitting at the windows.

"There once was a king," Cora said, a pain in her chest as if muscles were separating in her heart. "He had many daughters."

There once was a king. He had many daughters. An overbearing oldest by his first wife from an arranged marriage in his youth. He was somewhat afraid of this daughter, but it was she who saw to his needs as he aged and sometimes, when she wiped the corner of his mouth with a napkin, her touch was tender.

The next-born daughter, from a union with an enchantress who had seduced him when he rode in the forest, was sweet as the day was long, but when he tried to visit her in her tower in the neighboring town, her mother turned harpy, screeching and chasing him away.

His youngest daughter, by a pedigreed princess from a faraway kingdom, was the most beautiful and good, as all youngest princesses are. Nonetheless, she had disappointed him, spending more time inside her own mind than on affairs of state. And she had failed to wed, despite a miles-long line of suitors who camped year round outside the castle walls, littering the ground and creating a sanitation problem.

There was another daughter in the middle, but she was missing. In the fog of old age he had somehow . . . misplaced her. His memory of her was dreamlike. She had been by his side at a celebration, he didn't recall the occasion. Tents of sizzling food crowded the castle grounds, music and laughter ricocheted off stone walls. He had been happy, a sensation rare enough that he had noted it. His daughter had tugged at his hand, wanting to show him some thing of beauty she had found in the bordering wood.

At this point in his remembering, wisps of mist would once again descend and he couldn't recollect what had happened to her, why she wasn't with him any longer. He felt a vague sense of responsibility for her absence, a suspicion that he had done something he shouldn't, or failed to do something he should, but surely he would have protected her. She was his favorite, the one he parented perfectly, with no mistakes or scars. She was a composite of the other girls, their best parts with none of the back talk or baggage.

What had become of her?

The king's oldest daughter strictly monitored his visitors, but one day when she was occupied elsewhere, a man gained an audience. His robes were clean but had been mended more than once and the king distinctly heard his stomach growl with hunger. Taking pity, the king offered the man fruit from his own tray and asked, "What can I do for you?"

The man accepted the food, but said, after he swallowed, "Your majesty, it is rather what I can do for you."

The Puppeteer's Daughters

This struck the king as arrogant. He assumed the man was selling something and looked around for his oldest daughter to send him on his way.

"I can help you remember," the man said. "Any day you select will come back to you vivid and sharp. Your coronation, your victory on the battlefield, even the day you were born if you choose." The man listed these examples, and yet when the king blurted, "The last day with my daughter," he did not seem surprised.

The man untied a braided cord from around his waist and wrapped it once around his wrist then around the king's head in a circlet. The king felt a strange pulsing behind his eyes.

"Remember," the man said.

The king had long ago tamed the forest, driving out miscreants, thinning the trees so sun could dapple through leaves to the ground below. His daughter walked ahead of him. She tightened the knot of the kerchief that covered her hair, then trailed her fingers along the tops of bushes that flowered beside the path. The king sighed with pride at the lovely, interesting young woman she had become. The awkward years were behind her. She had come into her own.

"This is what I wanted to show you," she said, cupping her hands around a plant that grew in the hollow of an oak. "It's a four-leafed trillium. We shall have to call it a quadrillium." Her laughter was like wind chimes moving on a still day.

As the king bent to look, a man stepped out of the undergrowth onto the path. Ermine trimmed his black robe. Sun had carved laugh lines into his face.

"Well met, your majesty," he said.

The king's hand went instinctively to his sword, though the man did not appear to pose a danger. "You know me but I don't know you. Your name, sir?"

"Names matter little here," the man said.

"Was there something I can do for you, stranger?" the king said. "If you continue on this path you will find the celebration, if that is your destination."

"My purpose here is with you, and your daughter. You shall return to the celebration, and your daughter shall come with me."

"How dare you?" The daughter looked to her father to champion her.

The king drew his sword. "Be gone, rascal."

The man pointed to the trillium.

"Are you offended that I found this plant?" the daughter said. "I didn't even pick it. See? There it grows still."

"Look," the man said.

The king looked. In a drop of dew at the flower's center, he saw his other daughters as they went about their business at home.

"Either this one will come with me, or I shall pluck the trillium and take the other three." The man flicked the flower and the king saw his daughters stagger, as if the earth had quaked. His king's heart knew the man could carry out his threat.

"Are you a wizard?" the king asked.

"No."

"A bandit, then? Wanting my crown, my ring." The king removed his crown and ring but the man would not take them.

"Call me a bard. Or a messenger."

"What have I, or my daughter, done to attract your ire? Why do you say you must take her?"

"I harbor no ire. It is not that your daughter plucked a sacred plant, or trespassed, or your ancestors committed sins, or you didn't work hard or perform enough good deeds. It is simply the way of things."

The Puppeteer's Daughters

The king turned his wretched face to his daughter.

Had she been his youngest she might have gone willingly, to prove her goodness, but this middle child would have none of it. "Don't do this," she said, her brown eyes filling. "If you give me up, you will miss me every day until you die. I will be your ghost limb. The ache of me will wake you in the night."

"What choice do I have?" Tears streamed down the king's face. He could not deny the math—three of his children for one. His heart broke.

"She will be cared for," the bard said.

"But not by me," the king said, weeping.

The king bore it for a year, barely. At the end of the year he went back into the forest, which had grown wild with his neglect. He searched out the four-leafed trillium and called for the bard to come. Perhaps out of pity, the man appeared.

"It is too much," the king said. "I must have her back. Name your price."

The bard shook his head. "It is done. Once forfeited, such a child cannot be reclaimed."

"Then if I cannot have her, take away my longing," the king sobbed. "Make it as though I never knew or wanted her."

"Are you sure?" the bard said.

"Yes!"

So the bard took the cord that secured his robe, wrapped it once around his wrist and then around the king's head in a circlet. "Forget," he said.

The king found himself in his throne room. He recognized the shabbily dressed man before him as the bard from the wood, fallen on harder times.

"It is an age-old dilemma," the bard said. "Whether 'tis better

to keep striving or to pretend we never wanted what we seek. I am sorry."

The king stood, his muscles stiff. "If you will not return her, then I will search for her myself, even unto the ends of the earth."

"Why?" the bard asked.

"Because I cannot do otherwise." With that the king hobbled from the throne room, through the castle gate, and into the forest.

In the days that followed, his oldest daughter took the throne. His youngest finally chose one of the suitors squatting on the grounds and married. His second-born locked her harpy mother in their tower and moved into the castle to assist her sisters with the running of the kingdom.

From time to time, travelers would bring accounts of a man who might have been their father. They said he would greet them when they passed on the road, but would not stop. "Do you hear that?" he would ask and then be off, always following the sound of wind chimes moving on a still day.

Cora tugged her puppets off her hands. "I'm going to replace the bard with the raven. I'll say, *'Talking animals, while rare in the kingdom, were not unheard of.'* When the raven comes to the king in the throne room I'll say, *'The bird didn't look well. Its feathers were patchy, as if it had plucked some of them out of nervous habit. Its eyes were dull and watery. It had a chip in its beak. It seemed tired, as if it had flown a long distance without rest or proper shelter.'"*

"It's a heartbreaking story," Alice said.

Cora took the first sip of her gin and tonic. "I'm ready to sell. Go ahead with the Disney deal."

Chapter 43

Momentary lapses had happened before, sudden space where knowledge should be. Walter's gray matter was fraying, as was normal at his age, his brain no worse than a puppet in need of a refurb. New cloth, new foam, new glue would set him right, give him another twenty years of usefulness. Always before if he waited and didn't panic, the right thought or memory would show up like a guest held up in traffic and he would embrace it and hold it tight to be sure it didn't sneak off again.

Walter had flown down from New York to Raleigh because he preferred his Raleigh dentist. He stayed at the MacArthur Downs house, which he'd converted for use by visiting puppeteers after he divorced Luciana and settled her in an expensive condo in Miami. The MacArthur Downs property manager kept Walter's Mercedes SUV gassed up and ready for Walter and any other guests. Walter liked driving, something he rarely had a chance to do in Manhattan. He set out along the familiar route. He came to an intersection that the city had recently converted to a roundabout. Walter entered the roundabout, then could not remember how to exit.

He circled once, twice, waiting, but his mind remained vacant. He circled again, counting the spokes of the rotary but unable to remember what to do. He began to worry what it must look like, an old man chasing his tail. He set his face to look deliberate, intentional, as he waited for his mind to catch up and give him direction. Nothing came.

The turnoffs blurred by, humiliating him. His hands sweated and his foot cramped on the pedals. He felt as if he were in a high-stakes game of double Dutch jump rope. The ropes were turning, he was jumping, and he was supposed to duck out.

Finally, blue lights swirled in his rearview mirror. Blue lights meant pull over. He stopped the car with relief.

A young cop approached. Walter managed to roll the window down, found his wallet, handed over his license.

"Oh, Mr. Gray! Man, I love your puppets. I still have my old Zeno at my mom's house."

"Is that right?" Walter tried to smile.

"Somebody reported you going around and around the traffic circle. Is there a problem?"

"No problem. I was using it to think, like a meditation labyrinth." Walter hated his brain for being able to invent such a fine-hewn lie but otherwise failing him.

"Nothing illegal about that so I won't write you a ticket, but you might want to go ahead on so nobody else gets nervous and calls."

"I'll do that." Walter looked around, scoping out the exits, but had no more idea than before about how to be on his way.

His hesitation didn't escape the young officer. "How about I call somebody for you?" Behind him, other motorists squeezed past, gawking. Walter reluctantly gave the cop Jane's phone number.

She arrived with her son Brett. As she walked over to

Walter and the cop, the wind lifted her hair, showing gray at the roots. "Was there some issue with the car?" she said.

"No, ma'am. I think Mr. Gray got a little . . . confused. He was circling the roundabout for almost an hour."

"An hour?" She put a gentle hand on Walter's head as if checking a child for fever. Her solicitousness was harder to take than her normal impatience. He couldn't stand her treating him as if he were feeble, especially in front of his grandson.

"I got lost in thought, is all. Can we go now?"

Jane turned to Brett as if Walter weren't there. "I'll take him home and you drive his SUV. Come on, Dad." She thanked the cop and walked Walter to her car.

"So what happened?" she asked as they drove.

"Nothing."

"Dad. Has anything like this happened before?"

"No!"

"I'm going to make you a doctor's appointment. Sometimes infections can affect memory."

"I can handle my own appointments."

"Tell that to your dentist," Jane muttered, back to her old self.

At the MacArthur Downs house Jane followed him inside while Brett parked Walter's car in the garage. "Why don't you take a nap? You may just be tired. But I'd rather you not drive anymore while you're here, okay? I can take you where you need to go until we get you checked out."

"I don't need checking out."

"I'll try to get you in to see Dr. Stephens tomorrow."

So this was old age, Walter thought, when daughters ignored what you said and began to treat you like a child.

239

Not long after Jane left, Cora called. Jane had obviously put her up to it. "Hey, Daddy. Jane said you weren't feeling a hundred percent."

"I'm fine."

"Good. Jane's a worrier. But why don't you humor her and not drive anymore while you're down there? Driving's overrated anyway." Cora spoke in her I've-got-you-wrapped-around-my-pinky voice. Walter usually adored that voice, but today it made him want to smack her.

"Fine, if it will get you two off my back." In truth, he was afraid. He had no plans to climb back in that SUV.

He lay down for a nap, waking sluggish some time later to the sound of the doorbell. When he answered, a beaming Rosie stood there holding her daughter, Madison.

Anger flashed through Walter. "Jane sent you to check on me?" This was really too much.

"Jane?" Rosie looked confused. "We're here to take you to the arboretum. Are we early?"

And Walter remembered that he had made plans with Rosie, who wanted him to spend time with Madison. This new failing of his mind only upset him more.

"Are you okay?" Rosie said.

"There's nothing wrong with me!"

Rosie's face reddened. "Madison drew you a picture. You wanna give the picture to Papaw, honey?"

Madison buried her face in Rosie's ample chest. Madison was a toddler but Rosie had never lost her baby weight.

Rosie handed him Madison's drawing, a head with eyes and a line for a mouth, red crayon scribbled for hair. Its surrealism only made Walter feel more discombobulated. "Hey

240

Rosie, now's not a good time for me. I think I picked up a bug on the flight. Could we reschedule for next time I'm down?"

She was hurt, he could tell. She had dressed Madison up, in a frilly dress and little light-up tennis shoes, had curled the little girl's hair. He was such a shitty father and grandfather. He started to tell her he'd go after all, but she said, "Sure, it's not a problem. Can I do anything for you? Make you some soup or something?"

"No. I'll be fine." Walter touched Madison's arm. "We'll do something fun next time, okay sweetheart?"

Madison gazed at him with reproach.

After Rosie left, Jane texted him the time for a doctor's appointment the next morning, saying she'd pick him up.

Walter went to the locked study he maintained for his own use, where his gypsy princess marionette hung on her peg behind his desk. He lifted her down, plucked her strings to create a merry dance step. "*You* don't treat me like an imbecile, do you?" he said out loud. She rested her wooden hand on his forehead. He closed his eyes for a moment, taking comfort, before settling her back on her peg.

He kept a portfolio of vital papers in his desk drawer, including his will. He removed the will, running his hands over the fine paper. He recalled the satisfaction he had felt when he signed it, knowing it would protect Rosie from her evil stepmothers, and provide for all his girls. The wealth he had built from a silly blue puppet would free his daughters from financial worry forever. He remembered thinking even Jane would be content.

He ripped a sheet from a legal pad and spelled out "Cod-icil" at the top, digging the pen tip into the paper.

Forcing Jane to create a puppet was easy and satisfying. He almost spared Cora, but these men she allowed into her life—all dull as dirt, none of them able to truly demand her attention, pull her out of her own head. He needed to wake her up from the dream state she preferred.

As for Rosie, he felt suddenly affronted by her girth. How had his beautiful child let herself get so fat? Neither he nor Kiki were fat. Rosie had done this to herself, with lack of discipline and sloth. He would teach her a lesson like the others. It was for her own good.

With trembling hands he shoved the will and codicil into the portfolio. His elbow knocked his gypsy princess puppet. Her body swung against the wall so that she seemed to shake her head. Muttering, he turned her face away and limped to bed.

The next morning at his doctor's office he charmed his way through the mental status exam and was cleared to go. As he packed for New York, he remembered once with em-barrassment that he needed to tear up what he had written but then got distracted. The conditions remained in place for his daughters to fulfill.

Chapter 44

Cora had avoided talking to Jane since their meeting with Wilkie Bozer, still ticked off that Jane withheld the lab report, but she had no choice now. Jane was Walter's power of attorney. She voted his majority shares of Gray Steed. The minority shares were split among Cora, Alice, and Alf as part of their executive compensation.

"I have something to tell you that you cannot tell a soul," Cora said when Jane answered.

"Okay."

"Not a fucking soul or the SEC will be on us."

"Go ahead."

"I know you can keep a secret when you want to," Cora couldn't resist saying.

"Jesus Christ, Cora. Either tell me or get off the phone."

Cora told her about Disney.

"That's fantastic," Jane said. Cora had guessed correctly that Jane wouldn't feel nostalgia for the company, only resentment. But then Jane surprised her. "I want to come up when you sign the term sheet."

"It'll just be both management teams sending offers back and forth all day. Lawyers and investment bankers. It'll be easier if you authorize me to make the decisions."

"I won't interfere. I just want to be there. And Rosie should come too. A trip to New York will cheer her up."

"Fine. Bring a book to read. It'll be a long day."

"Great. Hey, can you ask Alice something for me? Brenna Mabrey told me Dad had set up an ongoing trust for Kiki to live at Lacy Street. I didn't mention it in front of Rosie because I didn't want her to blame Dad for Kiki not being in her life. It's possible he could have arranged something similar for a love child, with payments coming from Gray Steed."

"Sure, I'll ask her."

Cora walked down the hall to Alice's office. "Jane is coming to New York."

Alice's eyebrows rose.

Cora sighed. "She was there at the beginning, when Walter Gray was a few marionettes on the *Uncle Lee Show*. It's right that she should come. And Rosie's coming with her."

Alice nodded. "All right. I'll have my assistant book their flights and hotel."

"One other thing," Cora said. It was time to fill Alice in. "At his birthday party, Dad claimed he had a fourth daughter."

Alice's mouth dropped.

"I know, right?" Cora said. "It stunned us too. Jane wants to know if he set anything up through Gray Steed to support a child."

Alice shook her head slowly. "No. Nothing like that on our books."

"Thanks," Cora said.

꙳

CORA MET JANE AND ROSIE AT THE GRAY STEED RECEPTION desk when they arrived from the airport. Jane had gotten her boot off but still limped slightly. Rosie gazed at Walter's Czech marionettes in their glass display case. "I remember these little guys." She looked around the high-ceilinged lobby where the original Zeno and other Walter Gray puppets were mounted like artwork, along with framed photos of Walter with famous puppeteers and celebrities. "This place is gorgeous." Cora had forgotten that Rosie had never been to Gray Steed.

The elevator doors opened and Alf burst out. "Janey! Rosie! Cora told me you were here!" He hugged all three sisters to him, smushing Cora closer to Jane than she wanted to be. "Walter's girls, like the good old days. You have to let me take you to lunch."

"We'd love lunch," Jane said. Cora extracted herself.

"Great. Let's do twelve thirty. I can't wait to catch up."

"He's so sweet," Rosie said as they followed Cora to the elevator.

"He's in a bunch of Dad's old movies. I'll tell Pete to make him a copy," Jane said.

Upstairs they made a plan: Rosie would go shopping in Times Square. Cora and Jane would meet initially with the Disney management team, then leave it to Alice, the lawyers, and investment bankers to hammer out the term sheet.

Rosie left, excited to see the big city for the first time. Alice and Cora welcomed in a long line of men in suits from Disney. Once introductions were done and the real work of negotiation started, Cora and Jane excused themselves. Cora showed Jane to the workroom where Jane would hang out until lunch. Alice's daughter, Dee, was there, waiting for her nanny to pick her up.

"Do I need to do anything with her?" Jane whispered.

"No. Dee can entertain herself."

Glad to have her sisters out of the way, Cora went to her office, where Alice kept her updated all morning by text. It would be a straight-out stock purchase, all cash. Up for discussion were the valuation analysis, lock-ups, roles Cora and Alice would play after the acquisition, and Walter's movie.

Just as the Disney team declared a lunch break, Cora got a call from Dave Whitney, VP of feature film production at the Jim Henson Company. She wondered what Dave would say if he knew she was negotiating the sale of Gray Steed to Disney. She and Dave were competitors, but friendly. She let him tease her before he got to the point of his call. "I hear there's a shortage of plastic googly eyes in China. We're both fucked!"

"Not me. We're about to make a movie about puppet mole people," she said.

"Darn it, you bested me again!"

She laughed. "What's up, Dave?"

"Yeah, so. Professional courtesy. One of your employees has contacted us with a script. We're interested, but not if he has a noncompete."

"Who is it?" Cora said, miffed. The millennials Gray Steed had hired lately had no loyalty.

"Alf Anderson," Dave said.

"Alf?" That couldn't be right. Alf was as entrenched at Gray Steed as Cora was, maybe more so because he had worked for Walter for so long.

"I know, right? So, does he have a noncompete?"

246

"No," she said. "We don't make our employees sign a noncompete." Cora paid her puppeteers well, and gave them creative license to pitch any project. A job at Gray Steed was a prize. "What's his script?"

"Sort of *Princess Bride* meets *Bride of Frankenstein* meets *Bridesmaids*. Lots of brides."

"With puppets," Cora said.

"Lots of puppets. It's pretty hilarious, in a raunchy kind of way," Dave said. "He didn't bring it to you first?"

"He did not."

"Well I've gone and spilled the magic beans, haven't I? Don't tell Alf I called you. You know I like to shoot straight with you."

"Thanks, Dave."

When they hung up, Cora had to shake her head to clear it. Her father's oldest friend. Rage welled up inside her. She felt like a character in *Game of Thrones*. Or like Queen Elizabeth—the seventeenth-century redhead, not the nonagenarian occupant of Buckingham Palace. "Off with your head," she thought and then realized from the panicked look on the face of a passing intern that she had said the words out loud.

She texted Alice. *Are you alone? We need to talk.*

Chapter 45

Jane watched Dee make art with dried beans. Dee had sorted little piles: lima and kidney beans, black-eyed peas, elbow and honeycomb macaroni dyed spinach-green and carrot-orange. She was creating a face on a paper plate, careful dabs of Elmer's glue where the eyes and smile would go. She filled in a crooked red mouth with the kidney beans.

"That's cool," Jane said.

"I'm a good artist," Dee said. "You can copy me if you want."

"But I should make my own, right? Not copy you?"

"My moms say 'imitation is the highest form of flattery,'" Dee said. "People always copy me at school."

Jane suppressed a laugh. She peeled a paper plate from Dee's stack. When she reached for a lima bean she noticed a weakness in her grip; she supposed because it had been so long since she had used her pincer muscles—those used to hold a drawing pencil. She gathered various colored beans and pasta in her palm. She started to lay down macaroni eyebrows but was seized with a lack of confidence, an insecurity that she would do it wrong.

Dee used the honeycomb pasta to make hair. "What's the matter?" she asked.

"I'm not sure what to put down first," Jane admitted, frozen with dried beans in her hand.

"Eyeballs," Dee said. "My moms say 'the eyes are the windows to the soul.'"

Still Jane sat paralyzed. She remembered Pete and the boys at their dining room table with a project like this, macaroni spray-painted gold that they glued around a cardboard picture frame as a gift for Pete's mother, each boy's school picture pasted to the center. Jane was in the kitchen making dinner and feeling irritated about the mess. The three males were laughing.

"Do not get paint on my table," she warned them.

"Come help us, Mom," Brett said.

She could have joined them, had a moment of white glue and glitter, but she didn't even consider it. Instead she let herself be the odd person out, somehow enjoying that status. And the moment of small boys and laughter and pride in creation passed.

"Are you crying?" Dee asked, and Jane realized she was. She pressed fingers to her eyes.

"You can copy mine," Dee offered kindly.

"I was always better at drawing than beans," Jane said. She picked up a pen to do a quick sketch of Dee, confident that her hand would be sure, but when she set stylus to paper the lines didn't go where she wanted them to. She couldn't capture the soft curve of Dee's plaited hair or the determined set of her jaw. She had waited too long, and whatever gift she once possessed had atrophied. She set the pen down. "Excuse me, Dee. I have to make a phone call."

In the stairwell, she phoned Brett. "I'm calling to apologize," she said, her voice faltering.

"What for?" he said.

"For trying to squelch your creativity," she said.

"Mom."

"My father put his art before me. I swore I wouldn't do that, but I threw the baby out with the bathwater. I wish—I wish I had done crafts with you guys." She squeezed her eyes shut to stop the tears.

"Mom. We had Dad for that stuff. You held it all together. Kept Dad from spending all the money, made sure the toilet paper didn't run out, came to school to fight for me when they tried to put me in the 'dumb' class. You did okay."

"Really?" She wanted to believe it.

"Yes."

She wiped her nose.

"Come to my show Friday," he offered. "Nine o'clock at the Apple Peel. We're opening for Marcus King. Bring earplugs."

"Okay," she said.

"Awesome," he said.

Chapter 46

In fairy tales, trickery is often rewarded, but Cora was determined not to let Alf Anderson reap a reward from his betrayal of Walter Gray.

"I'm going to fire him," she told Alice. "I can't forgive him. All trust is gone. Fire him and claw back his stock before we sign the Disney deal."

They staged the confrontation before they summoned him: Cora behind her desk, her chair higher than the guest chair Alf would sit in, blinds configured so the sun would strain his eyes, Alice there as official witness.

Alf walked in all jovial, this man she had known since she was born, too loud, not as funny as he thought he was.

"Have a seat, Alf."

He sat. "All set for lunch? I made a reservation at the R Lounge—thought your sisters would appreciate the view."

Cora tapped her pen on her desk, then lay it down. "I got a call from Dave Whitney at Henson today."

Alarm twitched across Alf's jowly face.

"Oh yeah?"

"Yeah." She let the silence ferment. He shifted his body in his chair, blinking against the sun.

"He asked me to confirm that you did not have a non-compete with us, since he was considering partnering with you on a film."

Alf shook his head, looking down, his smile not a smile. "Can't get much past you, Cora. Listen, it was just a conversation. This is a little side project I've been working on. I didn't think Gray Steed would be interested."

"Would it not have been wise to try me?" she asked. "Would you have gone to Henson if my dad was still here?"

"That's just it, isn't it? Walter's not here anymore. I wanted to try something of my own."

"Did you develop it on my time?" Cora asked.

Alice chimed in. "If we check your computer history or the camera in the studio, will we find you working for Gray Steed or yourself?"

Alf didn't answer.

"I told Dave you did not have a noncompete. That we had never needed noncompetes. We could count on our employees to be loyal and not engage in conflicts of interest. You're free to work with him. You aren't free to work for me at the same time. I'm letting you go. Gray Steed will buy back your stock at face value per your employment contract. Alice will escort you to your desk and off the property."

"Co Co . . ." he beseeched. "You're overreacting. Please. I've been part of Gray Steed from the beginning, collaborating with your dad on every project he ever dreamed up. What would Walter say?"

Alice rose up out of her chair. "He would say 'Damn you, Alf. Why'd you go behind my back?'"

Alf turned on Alice. "Oh yeah? Behind *his* back? Why don't you tell Cora here how Walter was your sperm donor?"

Alice froze.

"What?" Cora said.

"That's right. Walter is Dee's father," Alf said.

"Fuck you, Alf, that is not your business!" Alice snapped.

Cora stared at Alice. "Is it true?"

"Yes," said Alice. "Though I don't know how this bone-head found out."

"Walter told me. Because I was his best friend. I was his best friend, Cora. Don't cut me loose."

"You're fired," Cora said, just as the door opened and Jane stuck her head in.

"Ready for lunch?" Jane asked. "Wait, who's fired?"

Cora rubbed her forehead. "Alice, walk Alf to his office, please." When Alice and Alf had left Cora smiled a fake smile at Jane. "Found our sister."

Chapter 47

Rosie hit Times Square. She had never seen so many people in one place in her life. Her neck hurt from ogling. Food beckoned everywhere. Halal trucks wafting roasted meat. Pizza dough bubbling. The M&M's store. Her stomach growled. She pulled a Ziploc bag of carrots from her purse and bit one. There was nothing as dull as a carrot. What she wouldn't give for a slice of Joe's Pizza instead.

Sometimes the whole promise of the gastric bypass seemed like a carrot on a stick, swinging on a fishing line in front of her without so much as a drop of ranch dressing. Though when she'd seen Nelson that week he'd been pleased. She'd lost sixteen pounds and kept it off. Her insurance had approved her to have the surgery once she lost forty. Nelson had given her the informed consent form to look at on the plane. She hadn't signed it yet, not able to read past the words "complications" and "death" and the warning that despite the operation, she might gain the weight back.

In front of Sephora, costumed characters posed for photos with tourists: two Elmos, a Spiderman, and a big blue Zeno. Rosie took out her phone and snapped a picture of Zeno for Madison.

Zeno bounded toward her with his furry hand out. "Where's my tip? No tip, no photo." The bass voice was gruff. The guy didn't even attempt Zeno's falsetto.

"Sorry," Rosie said. "I just thought you were cute. My father created Zeno."

"Don't give me that religious bullshit, lady. Where's my tip?" His costume was none too clean, the blue fur matted, as if it had been rented and never returned.

Rosie started to leave. He grabbed her arm. "Hey!" Rosie yelled. Inside the costume the man breathed hard. Zeno was supposed to be sweet and innocent. The creature in front of her had corrupted that, turned it ugly.

She jerked free. "Let go."

She pushed through the crowd and he gave up. "Fat bitch!"

Rosie walked far enough away that Zeno wouldn't harass her and sat down on a bench. She let her vision go blurry, absorbing the colors of stories-high electronic billboards hawking perfume, clothing, and Broadway shows. Light pulsed from the H&M Tower and TKTS booth. Car horns and sirens blared. People of every imaginable description flowed around her, speaking languages she could only guess at. She bet there was nothing in the world she couldn't find within four blocks of where she was sitting.

If only once, just once, her father had invited her to New York to see all this. But it hadn't occurred to him. She hadn't occurred to him.

It was time to come to terms with it. She hadn't been important to him, and truth be told he hadn't been a huge part of her life either, not like her mamaw or Gary. Both of whom were gone now. The inheritance would be nice, but being tangled in Walter's strings was only making her feel bad about herself. She didn't have time for that.

She took the informed consent form from her purse and called Nelson, pressing the phone to her ear so she could hear over the city noise that surrounded her.

"I've decided against the surgery," she told him.

"But you've worked so hard," Nelson said.

"I can't go through with it. I'm all Madison has. Gary loves her the best he can, but really I'm it. I can't do anything that would risk me dying."

"I respect your decision. I hope you'll keep up the healthy eating."

"I will. I promise." She would lose the weight for herself, however long it took. "Can I come by to see you once in a while to say hi?"

She could hear the smile in his voice. "Please come see me, Rosie Calhoun."

Rosie stood up. She had to head back to Gray Steed soon but wanted to find a souvenir for Madison first. She went into the Disney Store.

The Crabtree Valley Mall in Raleigh had a Disney Store, but it was nothing compared to this one. Two floors of merchandise. Mugs and shirts and princess gowns. Cookware. Candy. Unlike the costumed characters outside, the staff dressed as Disney characters were helpful and kind. Snow White stood on tiptoe to reach a crown on a high shelf for a little girl. Jasmine from Aladdin posed with a family of tourists without demanding a tip. Madison would love this place.

Rosie looked for something small that would be easy to carry on the plane. She chose a magic wand with tassels and a sparkly gold star on the tip.

Cinderella's fairy godmother worked the register, blue cape, gray wig, a Disney pin on her lapel that said "Bibbidi-Bobbidi-Boo!"

"Did you find everything you were looking for, dear?" the godmother asked as Rosie handed over her purchase.

"Yes ma'am."

The woman held up the wand. "Ah, good choice. This is an excellent wand. Full of wishes." She wrapped the wand in tissue. "You would be shocked—shocked!—at the number of people who don't use the wishes we fairies bestow. They let wishes molder like unused gift cards." She put the wand in a bag and handed it to Rosie.

"Thank you," Rosie said. She was almost to the door when the fairy godmother called after her. "Remember dear, always use your wishes!"

When Rosie returned to the Gray Steed lobby, Jane stood waiting, her arms crossed as if she were cold. The smile she gave Rosie was uncertain but real. "Guess what?" she said.

***

"HEY, DEE. I'M ROSIE, CORA'S SISTER." YOUR SISTER, ROSIE wanted to say so badly, but Alice had been adamant: she and her wife would decide what to tell Dee when she was older.

Rosie squatted down to Dee's level. She showed Dee a picture of Madison. "She's about to graduate from kindergarten. We're having a party. Maybe you and your moms can come down for it."

Dee shrugged. "Maybe."

Rosie wept for joy.

The Puppeteer's Daughters

"Why are you crying?" Dee asked.
"Because I'm happy," Rosie said.
"Your family cries a lot," Dee said.

Chapter 48

Cora held her raven puppet high on her arm, practicing its movements. She could feel Olin in the quizzical head-tilt and beating wings.

Alice knocked once and came in. Cora slid the raven off her hand.

"I'm sorry I didn't tell you, but Barbara and I wanted it private," Alice said.

"I can't believe I didn't see it. She looks like him."

A grin split Alice's face. "Doesn't she? That stubborn jaw."

"We'll recognize her as his daughter, of course. Dad has a will but we'll figure out how to provide for her. It can come out of my share."

"Absolutely not," Alice said. "He did it as a favor to me. We all agreed not to involve him beyond that. And no offense, but you three daughters don't seem all that happy. I've got my Gray Steed stock. We're set. But I do want her to visit your dad. Rosie invited us to the graduation party."

Alice checked a text on her phone. "The Disney team is back from lunch with a new offer. Here's what they'll pay if you stay on." She showed Cora the figure.

Cora chewed her cheek, a bitter taste lingering from the showdown with Alf. This was what she had become. Not an artist but a human resources drone. "How much if I don't stay?" she said.

"What?" Alice said.

"What if they get you, but not me?"

Alice stared at her for a long moment. "Is this because of Dee? Because I didn't tell you? You're mad at me."

"No! I love Dee and I love you. I want to . . . cut the strings."

Alice nodded. "I'll ask."

Chapter 49

Growing up, Jane sometimes wished Alf was her father. He was quick with a hug, the type of dad who would push a twenty dollar bill on his sons when they headed off on a road trip, check their tire pressure before they rolled out of the driveway. Walter Gray couldn't be bothered with such things.

Alf called her, blubbering, after security escorted him out. Jane went to Cora's office to plead his case. "I'm not saying keep him on. But let him keep his stock for the Disney deal. He deserves something."

"He stabbed us in the back," Cora said. "He stabbed Dad in the back."

"What if I don't agree to the term sheet?" Jane threatened.

"You would do that to me?" Cora asked, disgusted.

Jane closed her eyes. "No. I wouldn't. But one bad decision doesn't negate all the years Alf stuck with Dad."

"Doesn't it?"

"No! Nobody's perfect, Cora. People do selfish things, they hurt the ones they love. I'm sure he's sorry."

"I don't think he's sorry."

"I'm sure he is. Trust me. I know he is."

Cora crossed her arms. "All right. He can have his stock."

"Thank you," Jane said.

Cora picked up a puppet, a raven, from her desk and

played with it. Its shiny eyes glittered at Jane. "Alice wants you to know Dee won't make a claim on Dad's estate. You don't have to worry about your share getting smaller."

A few months ago Jane would have welcomed this news, but today it didn't bring her joy. "I like Dee. I'm glad we found her."

Cora gazed at Jane for a moment as if evaluating her. She set the raven down, opened the top drawer of her desk and slid a piece of paper toward Jane. "This is the certificate for my Gray Steed key employee stock. It's about to be worth a lot. I'm giving it to you. On one condition. You are never, ever again to complain to me or anyone we know about what *I* got compared to what *you* got when we were kids. You have to give that up."

Jane touched the certificate. Fingertip to paper. Walter's ship had come in after Jane left for college, but the fact was, Jane had the money she needed now. She made a good salary and lived beneath her means and could count on an inheritance when Walter died. How long had she nursed her resentment? It was a part of her, like a conjoined twin. The energy she had spent feeding it, making Cora feel guilty because she could. She lifted her finger. "No. You earned this money." She started laughing. "And I love complaining. Are you kidding me? It's my best thing! Buy yourself something pretty, kiddo." To herself she vowed to complain less in front of Cora, though she knew she wouldn't be able to give it up altogether.

Alice walked in. "I think we have a deal. They aren't interested in *Birdlandia*. They think the time for that has passed. But if you'll stay on for six months they'll give you your own pilot for your *Tangled Tales*."

"You got me a pilot?" Cora asked.

"Take it," Jane said.

"But no movie for Dad," Cora said.

The raven lay on Cora's desk, one watchful eye on Jane. The puppet was exquisite, Cora's artistry surpassing even Walter's. Jane cupped the bird in two hands and held it out to her sister. "Take the pilot."

Chapter 50

Cora pushed through the doors of Gray Steed headquarters onto the busy sidewalk, and exhaled a long breath. The term sheet was signed. She felt as if gravity had lessened around her. She would be free to do what she wanted, no longer tethered to the company. Now to decide what she wanted.

She walked to Columbus Circle and entered Central Park. She felt an urge to tell Sabine that she had found her sister, alive and well. That Madame Bea was wrong and should limit her predictions to ice cream from now on. But when she reached Sabine's bench the old woman wasn't there. Among a scatter of peanut shells, Cora caught sight of something red. Madame Bea's eye patch. She picked it up and brushed it off. Perhaps Madame Bea would see more clearly without it.

A soft wind picked up, rustling through grass and trees. In its sibilance Cora imagined Madame Bea's voice saying *I see what I see.*

Cora set the eye patch on the bench for Sabine to find the next time she came—if she came.

❧

IT WAS DUSK BY THE TIME CORA STEPPED OFF THE TRAIN IN Queens. The smell of roasting chicken from the Dominican place across from Olin's machine shop made her mouth water.

Olin was shutting off the lights in his shop. He looked up when he heard her come in. "Hey," he said with surprise.

How lucky am I, thought Cora, *to have this man look at me the way he does.*

His eyes scanned her corporate clothes and the layer of subway sweat on her face. "You just getting off work?"

"Long day," she said. "A good day, though." She told him about the Disney deal.

"What will you do?" he said.

"I'm not sure. But I think I would like to do it with you."

Olin took her hand. He led her next door to his apartment building, up the stairwell, past his landing to the roof. She wondered briefly about the legality of a machine shop with blow torches sharing a wall with a residential building, but this was New York. People worked where they could and lived where they could and asked for forgiveness instead of permission. Not her, but most people.

Olin pushed open the heavy metal door to the roof, which hung slightly crooked on its hinges and didn't close all the way. She saw a grill and two camp chairs, broken glass, a pile of cigarette butts. Then the view. Cora went to the edge and rested her elbows on the wall between splotches of bird droppings.

What was it about this city when the sun went down and the lights came on? The darkness erased graffiti, trash, rats. This high up you couldn't smell the garbage wind that blew up from soiled streets. The air felt fresh. Angled roofs formed pleasing cubist lines. She could look down into neighboring windows, see a woman doing yoga, a couple cooking together. Beyond the neighborhood, the Manhattan skyline leered like a boxer with his front teeth knocked out. Fast-moving clouds covered and uncovered an almost-full moon. "And I thought I had a nice view," she said.

Olin had nailed one of his sculptures, a small bird head covered with bottle caps, above the door like a ship's figurehead. She thought of his other sculptures, filling the back room of his shop. "Have you ever done an artist's residency?" Back before Walter left Gray Steed, Cora had spent an entire summer going from one artist colony to the next with other artists who had it down to a fine science, rarely paying room and board. She'd started with the National Puppetry Conference at the O'Neill and moved on to Hambidge, VCCA, McDowell, Yaddo. Getting in was validating. She got a lot of work done, though she tended to drink too much; the alcohol flowed.

"I don't do any of that," Olin said. "It takes too much energy away from the art." He flicked a piece of broken glass off the wall. "Do I need that kind of credential to be with you? Something that sounds impressive when you introduce me at parties?"

"No," she said.

"Because for you, I'd do it. Go live in a dorm and make small talk during vegetarian dinner and share a bathroom with a poet or something."

"Not necessary. I thought of it because you should have more time to sculpt."

"I make the time I need." Olin drew her to him, his embrace warding off the night's chill. "What will we do?" he asked.

We.

271

Chapter 51

M adison would graduate at ten o'clock on the kindergarten playground. Dew sparkled on the grass but it
promised to get hotter later in the day. Kids tore around like
wild animals. Rosie waited with other parents and grand-
parents for the ceremony to start.

Cora had brought Dee, and also a man, Olin. Just showed
up with him matter-of-factly as if bringing a boyfriend home
was something she did all the time. He seemed nice, though
maybe too serious. Jane had come, and brought her mother,
Ernestine. Ernestine had dug out her old yellow puppet,
Tino. They would convene at the Bevins nursing home after
the graduation, so Walter could be in on the party.

Madison was the only child in a graduation gown and
cap. She and Dee had made friends the way little girls do.
They took turns tapping each other on the head with the
fairy wand Rosie had brought back from New York.

Just as the teacher, Miss Anne, started to try to herd the kids
together, Gary's pick-up truck pulled up and he and Amber got
out. Gary slung a diaper bag over his shoulder. Amber unbuck-
led the new baby from its car seat.

Rosie watched them make their way across the lawn.
Amber wore what looked like boys' jeans, with her ponytail pulled back tight, glasses, and no makeup. She was as
skinny as ever—you'd never know she'd recently given birth.
Gary's upper arm touched Amber's as he adjusted the baby's

blanket. He absentmindedly gave the baby his pinky finger to grip and Rosie felt the bottom drop out of her heart. They looked like a family.

Madison ran across the lawn. "Daddy!"

He crouched to hug her. Rosie couldn't avoid speaking to them. She walked over to meet them.

"Hey, Rosie," Gary said, looking nervous. It offended Rosie that he'd be worried about her making a scene. She wasn't going to act ugly with Madison there.

"What a pretty baby," Rosie said with an aching throat.

"Thank you. He looks like his daddy." Amber jiggled from one foot to the other to keep the baby happy.

Rosie couldn't bring herself to look closely at the baby to see if he really did favor Gary. She'd have to work up to that. "Is he sleeping through the night yet?" she asked.

"Hell no," Gary snorted, but he didn't seem perturbed.

Rosie started to remind Gary of how they used to try to quiet Madison by driving her around in his truck, but then stopped herself. Amber wouldn't want parenting advice from Gary's ex.

Madison tickled the baby's foot where it stuck out from his blanket. Rosie's brain seemed to have locked. She couldn't remember the baby's name. "Madison, tell your little brother goodbye. It's time to line up."

"Can we have Madison this Saturday?" Gary asked. "Amber's family's having a reunion in Knightdale and we want them to meet her and Cody."

Cody. That was the name. Rosie looked down at Madison. "You want to?"

She jumped up and down. "Yes!"

"All right then. Go to Miss Anne." Rosie made the arrangements with Gary while Amber ignored her, all attention on the infant in her arms.

Miss Anne called out, "Parents! Gather around!"

Amber wandered over to a bench with the baby, away from the crowd.

"I'm going to be needing some child support," Rosie told Gary.

"Now come on, Rosie. We've never had to do that. You know I'll take care of Madison."

"You're going to have to be more regular about it. I can't wait around until you feel like slipping us a fifty." If Madison was going to college, Rosie needed to start an education fund.

Gary tried to sweet-talk her. "Baby, why don't I come by after a while and we can talk about it? You know we always have fun talking." He reached for her arm but she moved away.

"I believe I'm done with all that," she said, hoping it was true. "I'll have Madison ready for you to pick up on Saturday."

Gary headed to catch up with Amber, mumbling bad words.

A beat-up car stopped at the curb, driven by a man with prison tattoos covering the sunburned arm he stuck out the window. A woman with short brown hair got out. She looked around hesitantly when the car drove off. It took Rosie a second to recognize Kiki. Kiki started toward her, smiling, her false teeth strangely white against her leathery, hard-worn face.

"It felt weird to be in a car," Kiki said. "All the other cars were coming at us so fast. And nothing looks like it did. All the horse pastures are housing developments. I'd've got lost if I'd've drove myself."

"Kiki—Mama—I'm so glad you came!" Rosie almost cried. Kiki had left Lacy Street for her.

"We're starting, folks!" Miss Anne called.

Rosie took Kiki over to the crowd of adults that circled the slide. Before the actual graduation, Miss Anne led the kids in a song called "Whose Face Is On the Penny" to prove to the parents that their kids had learned something in kindergarten. Then, as she called out each child's name, that child climbed the slide's ladder and slid down, and Miss Anne handed them their rolled-up diploma.

When it was Madison's turn Rosie got her phone out to take photos, but Jane sidled up to her. "I'll take pictures. You watch it with your real eyes. She'll be grown before you know it."

"Madison Elizabeth Calhoun," Miss Anne called.

Madison held her magic wand high with one hand and bunched her graduation gown with the other so she wouldn't trip over it as she climbed the ladder. At the top she waved to Rosie before she slid down, the tassel on her mortarboard flying behind. Rosie couldn't have been prouder if it had been Madison's college graduation from Harvard.

"Isn't she cute as a bug?" Kiki checked her phone, one of those old-fashioned flip phones where you had to mash a key three times for each letter of a text. "Well, I did it. I left the rehab center and nothing bad happened. This is good. This is real good for me, Rosie. Thanks for inviting me."

"You're welcome," Rosie said.

"I'm heading out, honey." Kiki pointed to the street where the same man who had brought her idled in his beat-up car, smoking a cigarette.

"What, you're leaving already? Come to the party, Mama. I can drive you back after."

"I can't, honey. Temptation's always lurking. But this was good. Baby steps."

Rosie followed her to the street. Kiki got in the car and waved as it pulled away. Madison twirled up to Rosie. She tapped Rosie's shoulder with her wand. "What would you wish for, Mama?"

Rosie automatically quoted her grandmother. "If wishes were horses, beggars would ride."

"I know, but what if it was for real?" Madison said.

In fairy tales, the more specific a wish, the better, or the magic will find a loophole. Rosie could have wished for Gary's exclusive devotion, or tuition money for Madison, or a body transformed from fat to sleek, or a different history for her and Kiki. She could have crafted her wish with care and precision, anticipating every contingency. Instead, what welled up inside her was a formless, primitive prayer, for family and belonging and home. "Let's go find your aunties," she said.

Chapter 52

On the kindergarten playground, Ernestine tickled the chins of passing children with Tino's rainbow hair. She looked happier than Jane had seen her in years. Jane walked over and shook Tino's little yellow hand. "It's nice to see you again, Tino."

"Why *thank* you, Jane," Tino said. "Guess what? We haz a new gig!"

"You do?"

"Miss Anne wants us here on Wednesdays for puppet time!" Tino trembled with excitement.

"That's awesome. Will you be joining us at Bevins for the party?"

Ernestine lowered Tino and spoke in her own voice. "Nah. I'm still pissed at Walter."

Jane hugged her. "I'll stop by your place afterward. Bring you a plate." She waved goodbye to Rosie and Cora, telling them she'd see them at the party.

AT THE BEVINS ESTATE, JANE TUCKED THE SHOEBOX WITH THE *Amahl* puppets under her arm. In his customary place at the dining room table, Walter turned the pages of an old *Puppetry Journal* that Cora must have brought him. Cutlery clanked in the kitchen.

She kissed the side of his head. "Hey Dad."

He looked up and smiled. He pointed to the magazine page, an advertisement for a book about one of his heroes, Tony Sarg. "This is, this is, whatnot."

"Of course."

He turned the page. "And this is, this is . . ." He spiraled his finger over a black-and-white photo of an elderly Margo Rose showing another marionettist how to model a puppet's head. The magazine was from 1988. He had probably known every puppeteer featured on its pages. Jane wondered if he remembered any of them.

She set the shoebox between them and lifted the lid to show him the jumble of stick puppets. Three kings, a boy, a mother. The squares he cut with pinking shears for robes. Pushpin mouths. Sequin eyes, some fallen off as aged glue lost its adhesive. Loose Styrofoam balls: spares, or the heads of dead puppets, Jane wasn't sure which. "Remember these?"

"Amahhhlll." The word rolled down his tongue. Jane wished she had thought to find the music. Amahl's soprano might have evoked for him the memories it did for her. The two of them performing the opera together for Ernestine and Tino and Jane's stuffed animals. She and Rosie and Cora at various ages behind the hanging stage.

He reached out a trembling hand and Jane gave him Kaspar.

"Ahhhh." Walter touched Kaspar's head, crowned with gold braid, his robe a leopard skin remnant. The fabric store used to save Walter its best scraps. That's where he got the red denim he used for the *Amahl* stage curtain, thick enough not to unravel at the unhemmed edges. Once when Jane was mad at Walter for something she could no longer remember, he tried to bribe her with a particularly beautiful triangle of teal silk from the remnant bag to use for doll clothes. She blew her nose on it to spite him.

Walter made Kaspar bow, bringing the king to life. Jane could almost smell frankincense and myrrh over the dining room's food odors.

She found an extra stick at the bottom of the box. She covered it with a brown paper napkin from the dispenser in the center of the table and stabbed it into a Styrofoam ball. She handed it to him.

His lips worked. "You made a puppet!" He took the eyeless puppet and held it up, examining its porous skin. His tremor made the puppet shimmy. Jane cupped her hands around his to slow the dance.

Jane rarely let her mind turn to her early childhood, but the touch of Walter's skin invited an unexercised memory. Jane, perched on her father's shirtless shoulders. A campfire crackling, sparks bright against dark trees. Wood and marijuana smoke, her hands and Walter's hair sticky with toasted marshmallow. Strains of a guitar, adults tending other barefoot children. Her mother's face smiling up at Jane and Walter, Ernestine tickling Jane's knee with Tino's crazy hair. Jane grew cold and Walter set her down and wrapped her in the swath of black velvet he laid over his puppets when he was away from the van, to fool thieves into thinking there was nothing of value inside. He held the velvet snug and soft against her cheeks. "Janey, Janey, my lovely Janey."

Those gypsy camps between festivals were all she knew until a well-paying industrial commercial earned Walter the down payment on the Ginkgo Street house. Jane started school, where the children wore shoes and the type of shoe mattered. She learned to feel shame for her odd dad and overweight mother, who no longer looked at each other with delight.

What if they had stayed on the road?

Jane gently took the napkin puppet from Walter and laid it beside Kaspar. She pulled Walter's will and codicil from her purse and detached the codicil, working it off its staple so the paper didn't tear. "Could you destroy this for me, Dad?" He obliged, ripping it once, then twice into ribbons, looking for her approval. He arranged the pieces on his placemat, folding one strip over on itself again and again and pressing each crease. Jane watched him without speaking until he handed it to her, folded and small.

"Thanks," she said.

"Welcome," he said.

A staff member circled the table, offering Walter the day's menu and a pencil to select his order for lunch. It was a fiction the Bevins Estate indulged, a pretense that Walter and the other residents could still choose for themselves. Walter's hand rested on his paper placemat. Jane took the pencil and traced his fingers. She added creases where his fingers bent, cross-hatched the shadow between thumb and pointer. At first she faltered, hesitated, erased, but her strokes became more sure. Muscle memory awakened and her pencil glided over the paper. Her father pointed and laughed, a high giggle as she drew.

Cora and Olin entered the dining room, carrying trays of food for Madison's graduation party. "Recreation room, right?"

"Yes, through there." Jane swept the pieces of the codicil into her hand and dropped them into a nearby trash can. She pulled Walter's chair out from the table. "Here Dad, stand up. It isn't too far for you to walk."

Chapter 53

In fairy tales, people live happily ever after.

The sisters—all of them now—milled around Walter, who sat in an easy chair in the recreation room's soft lamplight.

Olin bent to shake Madison's hand, formally congratulating her.

Madison craned her neck to look up at him. "You're tall."

"Haven't you ever met a giant before?" Olin asked her.

"There's no such thing as giants," Dee said.

"Are you sure?" Olin said.

"Are you a good giant?" Madison asked.

"If you mean, do I eat little girls, no. I'm a vegetarian."

"Could you lift me up?" Madison held out her arms. Olin lifted her into the air with no effort and touched her head to the ceiling. She squealed long and loud in delighted terror.

Dee bounced up and down. "Do me!" Olin set Madison down. He picked Dee up, swooping her toward the floor then over his head. "I'm flying!"

Jane elbowed Cora. "He's showing off for you."

Cora touched the star hanging at her throat. She loosened her ponytail and shook out her flaxen hair. "Your point?"

The recreation room doors opened and a man shuffled in. Wilkie Bozer, the genealogist. "What's he doing here?" Cora asked.

Mr. Bozer crossed the room toward them. He looked better kempt than the last time Cora had seen him: his green cardigan free of lint and paper bits, nails neatly clipped. He had apparently discovered depilatory to manage his ear hair.

"Ladies," he said, bowing slightly. "And Mr. Walter Gray. What an honor, sir."

"Can we help you?" Jane asked him.

"Forgive the intrusion. You'll recall at our meeting I told you of my preference for documentary research over genetics. Your case has stayed on my mind. I did a bit of snooping at the courthouse yesterday and found this, which I thought might interest Rosie." He held up a document.

"What is it?" Rosie said.

"It's an Affidavit of Paternity signed by Mr. Gray, paternity test attached. See? 'I the undersigned, being duly sworn, freely and voluntarily declare and acknowledge that I am the natural father of the child named herein.' That child would be you, my dear."

"The paternity test was me?" Rosie asked.

Mr. Bozer handed the Affidavit to Walter. "Do you recognize your signature, sir?"

"Careful, he'll tear it," Jane warned, but Walter smoothed the paper on his lap. He looked up. "Rosie," he said.

"Yes!" she said.

"My Rosie," he repeated. Rosie's face pinked with pleasure. Walter held the document out to her. She accepted it and hugged it to her chest.

Cora opened her purse. "Mr. Bozer, let me pay you for your services."

"No, no. No charge," he said, though he looked tempted.

"A piece of cake, then," Rosie offered.

He waved a hand. "You're kind, but I must be going. If I can assist you in the future, with anything at all, don't hesitate to call."

With another little bow he left. As the door shut behind him, simultaneous texts chimed. Jane, Rosie, and Cora checked their phones.

"It's Gene23 with our test results," Jane said. "Three hits."

"Same," Cora said. "Guess what—we're sisters."

Madison and Dee had found the shoebox of *Amahl* puppets and spread them out on the floor in front of Walter's chair. Jane explained who each character was. When Dee held the three kings up to perform, Walter leaned forward. "Your hands!" he said to Dee. "Your hands are like my hands!"

It was true—Dee's small hands with their flat nails were his in miniature. Envy seized the other daughters for one wild millisecond, then disintegrated like aging puppet foam. Jane felt her shoulder muscles loosen.

"Take a picture of us with Dee, Olin." Jane handed him her phone.

The daughters surrounded Walter's chair. As soon as Olin snapped the shots, Dee sprinted away to play with Madison.

Olin returned Jane's phone and she showed the photos to Walter. "There, Dad. All of your daughters together."

Walter's brow furrowed. "No," he said. "One is missing. Where is she?"

The adult sisters looked at each other. Jane shook her head.

"Here we go again," Cora said.

"He's just confused." Rosie nudged a bite of cake onto a fork and lay it down resting on the edge of a plate. She touched the back of Walter's hand. "Eat, Dad."

THREE HUNDRED MILES NORTH, AT THE SMITHSONIAN, A CON-servator stood before a replica of Walter Gray's marionette bridge, comparing his work to a photo from Ginkgo Street. Already hung were a long-legged frog, the soldier with his tinderbox, and the conjoined princesses with their long golden hair. Other puppets lay in mounds in their boxes. The conservator went to lunch.

A single puppet lay half in, half out of her box. Her red kerchief had slipped off her cropped black hair and covered one eye. She straddled the edge of the box, as if preparing to run for the forests and the fairgrounds in search of a father she had missed.

In the Bevins Estate recreation room, as his family mingled around him, Walter spread trembling fingers, working familiar, beloved strings only he could see. Hand-shadow danced in the lamplight, leaping large across the wall.

"There's another one," he said, forlorn. "Where is she?"

Acknowledgements

Thank you to my agent, Pamela Malpas, and the team at Turner Publishing for embracing this book. I'm grateful to the puppeteers who answered my questions and helped educate me about the magical world of puppetry, especially Keith Shubert, Hobey Ford, Phillip Huber and David Syrotiak. Thanks to Victor Gao and Jon Blumenfeld for a crash course in corporate mergers and acquisitions, and to my mom Suzanne Newton for letting me use her Bait & Tackle joke. Deep gratitude to all the readers who gave me feedback along the way, especially those who were willing to read the whole novel during a pandemic: Flatiron Writers Alli Marshall, Marjorie Klein, Tessa Fontaine, Maggie Marshall, Kim Mako, A.K. Benninghofen, Catherine Campbell, Maryedith Burrell, Joanne O'Sullivan and Jude Welchel; Suzanne Newton, Michele Newton Dohse, Sonja Dohse, Katja Dohse, May Castelloe, Lynda Mottershead, and Julia Hegger.

Book Club Discussion Questions

1. Now that you've read the novel, go back and reread the epigraph. Why do you think Newton chose this quote? Who do you think are Walter's beloved dolls?

2. Which sister (Jane, Rosie, or Cora) appeals to you most and why? Which sister do you think changes or grows the most by the end of the novel? How do the sisters' relationships with their father, and with each other, change throughout the novel?

3. What do you think of Rosie's "twig house" relationship with Gary?

4. Thievery is a theme in this novel, as is often true in fairy tales. What are some important thefts in the book? How do the thefts affect the thieves and the victims? Why do you think Cora's thefts stop?

5. What do you think Walter's gypsy princess marionette symbolizes for him?

6. What are the respective attitudes of Jane, Cora, Rosie, and Olin toward creativity and claiming a creative life? In what ways (if any) do you think Rosie is creative?

7. In Cora's story, "The Sound Seeker," the Sound Seeker can find lost words. What are some words in your own life that have been lost which you wish you could retrieve?

8. In Cora's variation on the story "Diamonds and Toads," the Reverser of Curses makes the following statement about curses and blessings: *"It can be hard to tell the difference at times. These things have two sides, and the side one sees has more to do with the seer than the seen."* Do you agree with this statement? Why or why not?

9. Jane's friend Avril says, "At some point, we all have to appreciate what our parents did give us and stop resenting what they couldn't." What do you think Walter was able to give his daughters? What do you think he failed to give them? In your own relationships with your parents or children, what has been given? What has been withheld?

10. Fairy tales often feature encounters with strange folk who are not what they seem. What are some examples of these encounters in the novel? What do you think is the significance of each?

11. What memories do you have of puppets from your childhood?

About the Author

HEATHER NEWTON is a practicing attorney, a creative writing teacher for UNC Ashville's Great Smokies Writing program, and co-founder and program manager for the Flatiron Writers Room in Asheville, North Carolina. Her novel *Under The Mercy* Trees won the Thomas Wolfe Memorial Literary Award and was named an Okra Pick by the Southern Independent Booksellers Alliance. Her short story collection, *McMullen Circle*, was a finalist for the W.S. Porter prize. *The Puppeteer's Daughters* is her second novel.

CPSIA information can be obtained
at www.ICGtesting.com
Printed in the USA
JSHW032003160223
37848JS00001B/1